IRO's MERMAID

IRO's MERMAID

Tanvi Singh

AMARYLLIS

AMARYLLIS
An imprint of Manjul Publishing House Pvt. Ltd.
• C-16, Sector 3, Noida, Uttar Pradesh 201301, India
Website: www.manjulindia.com
Registered Office:
• 2nd Floor, Usha Preet Complex, 42 Malviya Nagar,
Bhopal 462 003 – India
Distribution Centres
Ahmedabad, Bengaluru, Chennai, Hyderabad,
Kochi, Kolkata, Mumbai, Noida, Pune

Iro's Mermaid by Tanvi Singh

This paperback edition first published in India in 2026

ISBN 978-93-7317-061-9

Cover design: Trinankur Banerjee

Printed and bound in India by Repro India Limited

'This is the way the spirits talk...'

THE MAN WHO MARRIED THE MOON

'It is said that whenever anyone on the first island passed away, their souls walked a cane bridge none could see—a bridge that connected the land of the living and the land of the dead. But there was one soul who refused. Can you guess who it was, my moonchild?' Piribi asks her granddaughter, Iro.

'You, Maa-ji?' Iro whistles, flashing a proud toothless grin.

'I still have a long life. Silly child. Now, listen closely, Irah, for the beings I tell you about will come for you one day when you call.'

There was no night or day, no sun or moon, nor any wind or fire... Piribi begins, narrating the tale of her ancestors.

Just an endless ocean in which the gods lived, always surrounded by a perpetual cloud, when the very first of the lands rose above the water. An island with nothing but a single Jarul sapling growing at the heart of it, sustained not by the sun, but the darkness around the world. Let us call this island the Big Island, shall we, my moonchild? Soon, countless others followed, teeming with life. But not the first island, where neither the beat of a wing nor the hum of an insect could be heard.

As the sapling grew into a tree, the clouds dissipated, and the sun, who had never seen a land quite as lush, turned its gaze to the earth, bathing the world in buttery-yellow light. It did wonders for the land! My Baba told me that extraordinary creatures of the deep sea would travel inside a thick cushion of sea foam and come to rest on the shores of the Big Island, an island so full of life... yet, not one with its own heartbeat, of course.

Or at least, a heartbeat we don't know.

A glorious crop of Kobo bushes and myrtle trees sprang up from this Jarul sapling, covering the whole land. It was the Life Tree, of course. Strong creepers bent low, weighed down with bright fruits, ripe and delicious. There were reed-like bleached spruce barks dotted with amber resin, thick and sturdy shoots bearing green cardamom pods sprinkled with little black seeds, their mouth-watering fragrance wafting all the way to the nearby islands, and ruffled flowers that glowed like stars none had seen the likes of. The stillness in the air held an anticipation, almost as if the island lay in wait. Then one day, the stillness broke.

With each sun drop, the Jarul trunk grew fatter and fatter. Odd, isn't it?

You see, inside the trunk of the now mighty Jarul tree, an egg was slowly growing. It wasn't just a normal egg, you know, but opal-like and speckled with gold. When lightning struck the island, following a fight between Moïco, the god of fire and Tarai, the god of water—they did have plenty—it struck the tree as well, splitting it right down the middle, and out fell the speckled egg.

Now, a normal egg would break. But not the Jarul egg. It rolled down into the soft grass and came to rest in a bed of pink Jarul petals, where it hatched. Out came not a bird, as one would think, but a little boy with gold eyes and skin like earthen pots. He was so tiny, you could hold him in your palm!

Yul, the goddess of wind named him. The guardians and deities who had watched this remarkable incident unfold said that the tree grew with the speckled egg already placed in its trunk when the island rose—a child of the mighty whale upon whose hump the world balanced, hidden inside the tree trunk to keep him safe from Moïco and Tarai. But none could find the great whale, and Yul was left alone.

Though small of body, Yul had a heart as strong as his parent tree. He crawled to safety in the same Jarul. Alone, but not scared. Being a child of the ocean, Yul grew fast. Too fast. Soon, he made a little hut, and from the same Jarul branches, he made a small bow. But you see, little Yul wasn't as alone as he thought. A million others gathered around him, drawn to this new life as its watchful protectors.

Mite, the mighty dove, sent her children to swarm the sky. Their robust feathers broke the strength of the worst of downpours, keeping at bay the drongos, the long-tailed omens of the underworld. Myia, the great blue prawn, urged the sea creatures—from the tiniest molluscs to the majestic whales—to surround the island and stop the waves from washing him ashore as little Yul learnt to fend for himself.

Seasons passed, and little Yul grew to be as mighty as the Jarul tree he had hatched out of. A fine bearded man he had become, protecting the creatures that had once protected him. The creatures were always around to keep him company, and yet, Yul felt something was amiss.

One day, strolling on the rocky beach, Yul came across a clamshell glowing in the phosphorus sun. Right before his eyes, the shell opened up and out fell a little pearl. Now this pearl was the most beautiful thing Yul had ever laid eyes on. Gazing at it admiringly, how he wished the creatures and the gods too could see its delicate beauty! He wandered along the beach until dusk, watching the world plunge into darkness. He knew what he had to do.

Swinging his arm upwards, Yul threw the pearl as high as he could, sending it soaring above. Then all at once it stuck, stitched in the sky, growing bigger and bigger till everyone could see it. Yul was awestruck. He looked on in awe as his creation bathed the world in its luminous, ethereal glow. He reached out with one hand to touch it, but stopped when he saw someone walk down the moonbeams and come to stand in front of him. Tuya, a woman as sublime as the sky pearl, and the keeper of the moon. The magic of the moment filled his heart and Tuya soon became Yul's wife.

For a thousand turtle years, they raised their children, and their grandchildren, and then their grandchildren's children... and so forth when they met the other islanders, teaching them everything from rowing to hunting to weaving.

Until one day, when the sun shone brighter than ever, Tuya left for the skies.

I need to, she said in despair. The moon had begun to dull without her. The sun was forced to shine brighter to sustain the moon in the absence of its keeper, and now the gods were worried that the sun's brightness would burn the earth.

Grief had no limits, Yul came to realize, growing older in years but not in body, till the world no longer remembered Tuya, the keeper of the moon, and Yul's world. Yul wished to join her, but other things demanded his presence.

A war broke out between Moïco and Tarai. Their rage levelled the earth. Great floods came, consuming one island after another.

Distraught and terrified, Yul prepared to leave to resolve the tiff between the gods. He urged the mighty dove Mite to keep his children safe when he was gone.

I wish you the best, brave Yul, said Mite. I shall watch over your children as I had watched over you once.

His children hid in Mite's nest, surviving on the berries and seeds strewn inside, with the fire Tarai kept hidden by his side their only hope of survival.

This fire was a prized drop of the sun that had fallen to the bottom of the ocean where Tarai had found it. The great ocean god was mesmerized by this fire drop that, miraculously, hadn't extinguished. How could it, for it was the very essence of the fire Moïco had placed in the sky to light the world? The fireball grew tired the longer Tuya remained on earth, until it could take it no longer.

Give the fire to the children of Yul, great god Tarai... Myia, the majestic blue prawn, had urged Tarai in a meet among the gods and guardians of the islands before Moïco and Tarai declared a war. *Let them flourish. They shall build a world we can't even imagine.*

None shall have my gift from the sun, roared Tarai, *which you wish to steal from me! Moïco has gotten to you, hasn't he? He is the god of fire. Ask him to give the children of Yul his fire.*

Moïco is the one who put the fire in the sky, great god Tarai. The fire belongs to him, Myia explained. *And you have kept the soul of the fire locked in the ocean. How can he give it to the children of Yul?*

His fireball lost its soul because of the keeper of the moon, came the strident reply. *Her children suffer because of her. I found the soul, and I shall keep it.*

Disappointed, Myia retreated to the crevices below the ocean bed, and vowed to come out only when Yul's children called for him.

When Tarai called Moïco to war, he left the fire unattended, for who could ever swim to the depths of the ocean to retrieve it?

The fire would save the children of Yul, the guardians

knew. But none could get close to Tarai's home, except for Myia. They were guardians of the land and sky, not the great ocean, you see.

Upon hearing the cries of Yul's remaining children, Myia escaped the depths of the ocean with the fire, but lost it when Totemo, the crafty kingfisher, stole it from him in an attempt to overthrow Mite as guardian of the sky.

Totemo hid the fire in his beak, but he had underestimated the strength of the soul of the sun. The fire scorched his throat till the feathers on his neck turned a violent crimson. Unable to bear the heat, Totemo threw the fireball out just as he was flying above the first island. But before the fire could touch the dry leaves of Mite's nest, Mite caught it, singeing her ivory feathers bronze, and gave it to Yul's children, thus finishing Myia's task and ending the war.

And Totemo? For his disgrace, Moïco cast him into the fireball in the sky, saying he would only be able to return to earth as a firebird if he repented.

But Yul was inconsolable, caring neither for the gods nor their wars. Rueful, Moïco and Tarai apologized for the destruction their rage had wrought. But Yul's time on earth had come to an end; it was only supposed to last until that very moment.

No need for Ferriers of the ocean to guide you. I shall walk you over the cane bridge instead, brave Yul. The great god of afterlife awaits, said Tarai, ashamed. I can't change the ways of fate, but know this—you shall forever be worshipped.

The afterlife won't have Tuya, Yul replied. I do not wish to be treated like the gods, great Tarai. Give me a place beside the keeper of the moon where we can watch over our children. Task your Ferriers to give them a safe passage over the cane bridge when their time to meet the great god Côl comes. Let my sorrows not be passed onto my children, but let them find joy where one might struggle to. That is all I ask of you.

Very well, Moïco declared, a god of few words but abundant with blessings. He gave the gentle-hearted Yul a place in the skies for eternity where he could live beside Tuya as the brightest star.

It is said that Yul calls the skies his home now, bringing in daylight every day, while Tuya ushers in the night as the two watch over their children to this day. As for their children, Moïco and Tarai tasked Myia and Mite to watch over them as doting guardians, a task they diligently—

'Irah? Oi!'

Piribi pauses. Iro had fallen asleep halfway through the story. She nudges Iro's short messy curls off her forehead. Stars in the skies, she called her hair, a head full of silver on a child so small. My moonchild...a child of the keeper of the moon. Piribi ruffles her hair once more, and covers her legs with the rumpled cotton sheet Iro had kicked away.

Piribi stands, and goes to look out of the window. Iro's soft snores are the only sound that breaks the silence. The quiet would last an hour more, that's all. She raises her palm towards the green light coming from the newly built lighthouse on the Big Island. *Her old home.*

Iro had asked Piribi to tell her the tale of Yul—Iro's first ancestor, and Piribi had happily obliged. Of course, neither the ancestors remained, nor the essence of the island. But Piribi did believe that even though they were now away from home, everything and every being's heart was steeped with the island's magic, and the ancestors and deities would answer when called.

At least she hopes they will.

THE GIRL WHO LIVES IN THE CLATTERING HOUSE

'Beyan! Koio!'

Iro calls out toward the dense forest behind her house and waits, tapping her little toes in the warm white sand. As she hums Piribi's songs, she drags her bare feet to draw sickle moons till they look like the kobo bushes in front of her. She has timed her schedule perfectly today.

Once her father, Tebishiro, left for the Big Island, out came Iro's little wooden frame from the shed. She propped her round coracle boat—Dongi, she called it, made by Tebishiro upon her request—on the frame, securing it with rough jute ropes, and inspected everything inside. A large net she had made with her own hands, a straw pot for her catch, a small box containing brightly painted baits, and of utmost importance, secured inside a large banana leaf and neatly tied with a twine, her lunch. Rather full from the hearty congee Tebishiro made for breakfast, and buzzing with energy after her Maa-ji's tale about Myia, Iro is on a mission.

A mewl sounds in the distance as the ruffled palm fronds

begin to rustle. Two fluffy civets come bounding up to nuzzle Iro's hand before scampering off to their chosen spots, standing unmoving as she tethers them to her landboat. The wide brim of her straw hat dusts her frail shoulders as she climbs into her Dongi. Iro grips the harness tight, and off she goes. The busy port of Enmei lies waiting.

❖ ❖ ❖

A small island, not too different from others in the eastern archipelago to the mainland, surrounded by a calm turquoise lagoon, the white shores of Enmei are a paradise. Yet, according to Old Man Ehri, Iro happens to be the chaos that lies underneath his island's idyllic beauty. But he would say that, wouldn't he?

Iro is small for a child her age, and prefers to find leisure in her little round boat, fishing with all the comfort of a rich merchant and not a care in the world. Some days, Iro simply scours the sand for shells, making pendants and charms as tall as herself to hang around her house's beams, and those of Poi—her family's restaurant and delivery service. By now, she has covered almost every inch of the beams in shell pendants, making the structures loudly clatter every time the winds pick up. Tebishiro believes the beams will give out one day. Nevertheless, he still encourages Iro, fishing out empty shells in droves for her. If not the beams, then the trees it is.

The calm inland waters of Enmei are abundant with sea life. Small boats and ferries laden with freshly caught fish the size of kayaks, bright, fragrant fruits and small coconuts with the tint of setting sun, and sometimes, perhaps the most coveted ones—large barrels of fish oil, leaving for the Big Island's red and white harbour each morning. Iro runs to see them off, jumping and waving at Tebishiro from Enmei's pier till his ferry is but a dot in the distance.

At one time, Tebishiro, along with the men from her village, used to leave for the Big Island regularly, seeking work. They said the foreigners—the men in uniforms—needed more hands to construct the city they were building for themselves over there. But Tebishiro didn't help build the city. Rather, he fed the ones working there.

Big boats the size of twenty whales piled on top of each other, Tebishiro exclaimed one evening at dinner, back home after a tiring day, his dark eyes going wide as he recounted seeing the ship docked at the Big Island's harbour on the other side. Iro had listened to him intently, her meal—two meagre cuts of fish and short sticky rice swimming in watery, rundown curry—getting colder.

'I have never seen anything like it. They have large nets which take everything to the inner lands to feed more of their uniformed people. None of it is for us, I tell you. Soon, we will have nothing.'

Though she can't understand much, Iro knows the big boats and men in uniform are responsible for her parents' grim faces. But she does hear hums of disapproval coming from her grandmother every time they talk about them.

Ah, there it is again, the familiar hum from Piribi, who sits by the cooking pot, stoking the embers with a long stick.

❖ ❖ ❖

Iro's grandmother had been one of the few ancestors in Enmei who had reached the little island with just a roll of clothes and a seven-year-old Tebishiro by her side when the people with shiny badges and crisp uniforms came to her island.

The tales of the men in uniform in the mainland had reached the archipelago when Iro was to be born. These visitors had been there for a long, long time before anyone from the islands ever saw them, arriving in majestic ships that gleamed in the sunlight, their masts robust and starch white. They walked in single file with their rifles poised upon their shoulders, proudly on display for one and all. Skin as pale as the sand of Piribi's home and speaking words they couldn't understand, the people in the mainland had said these visitors were going to stay for a long time.

They had been right.

Soon, the uniformed men brought along their families. The city slowly grew, but the same couldn't be said about the natives. No adzes were a match for the raining fire from the shining ships' sterns and the uniformed men's bayonets. Those who could leave did, some stayed to fight and became the island spirits, and the ones who remained? They became the very first of the fettered men to be taken to the Dark Place.

The Big Island, now called the Wallis Island, established itself as a major port in the Eastern Sea, drawing in trade. But not for the natives, who needed a permit to conduct business if they were allowed, and shell out even more for the visits. For those were expensive. After all the expenses and tributes, Tebishiro barely had money left over to buy just enough rice for their restaurant.

You needn't worry about your family, Piribi would say. Iro and she were excellent foragers. Their island's abundance was enough to nourish them.

But how long will foraging sustain them?

Tebishiro lacks the faith and joy his Ma has. Why wouldn't he? Piribi hasn't witnessed how they run the Big Island. Hope and faith dissipate the moment one sets foot on the stone pier, he has seen that. Tebishiro is ever so restless. Yet, the clatter that greets him each time he comes home comforts him. Perhaps, that is why Iro hangs so many pendants and charms around the house, just to see Tebishiro smile.

However, this Big Island is something Iro remains most curious about. Some nights, her grandmother mumbles that the spirits of her people will haunt the new people of the island. There would be so many of them now, as tall as the trees and glowing a faint spectral blue.

And some nights, watching from her house, Iro can see the dull rays of light coming from the Big Island, the newly constructed lighthouse on the far east guiding boats to it. She puts her small palm out and tries to catch the fractured beams, utterly mesmerized by it.

'Just there...see, Irah?' Piribi would point towards the green light emanating from the island. 'That is where Myia lives.'

'How come no one has seen him then, Maa-ji?'

'Myia is smart, my moonchild,' Piribi would say with a knowing smile. 'He is everywhere, dispersed into the water as the translucent crabs. He needs to rest. Remember that. Whenever he is needed, all those crabs will join together to recreate Myia.'

'That's not what you said last time!' Iro would protest.

'What *did* I say?'

'The pig with a fish tail swims to the ocean bed and wakes Myia.'

'Which story do you like more?' Piribi asked.

'The pig.'

'Well, have your pig, then.'

❖ ❖ ❖

Maa-ji. That's what Iro calls Piribi. Her grandmother is a small woman, with ever-present frown lines on her gentle face. She walks with a hunch, wearing a faded crimson wrap skirt and tunic she had woven on a rather ancient loom, wearing heavy bead necklaces that have begun to weigh her down, and sometimes, she smells funny.

'I am old. Old people do smell,' she chides the girl whenever she asks about the peculiar smell that floats about her, just one of a whole flood of questions she has prepared.

But her favourite ones are the stories of the great blue prawn, stories that her grandmother's grandmother used to tell. Many is the time when Iro has tried to find this great prawn, taking her small, trusted coracle boat, and sailing in it almost to the brink of the calm lagoon where a strong stone barrier guards the island.

And that is where her adventures stop.

Do not sail over the lagoon, Iro, Tebishiro had warned her.

She knows what could happen if she tries to go over the brink and into the open ocean. Sometimes, desolate pieces of boats would be seen drifting off to their shore.

See what happens when Moïco gets angry, Piribi would say with a frown. Iro knows it's not Moïco. The great god of fire is kind. Many a boat has been downed by fire raining from the sky near the Big Island—fire from the cannons of the new ships the Big Officer brought with him. And that terrifies her.

Sometimes, Iro skirts the very edge of her lagoon from where she can see the big ships moored by the Big Island, taking her small net and trying to determine if each crustacean she caught is the fabled Myia or not, worried she might have eaten him by mistake.

You can't just eat Myia, my moonchild, Piribi laughs.

Iro tries to ask Piribi about the Big Island, but the old

woman merely smiles at her, her wrinkled, tawny skin creasing even more. When she does speak, she simply says she's content. That the Big Island holds nothing for her that Enmei hasn't already gifted her.

All Piribi has of her home now are the fables that have found their way into little Iro's heart, fables she believes to be true. Isn't that what Piribi had intended, after all? To just have at least one of them believe, one of them be hopeful?

And some nights, Iro dreams of hoisting those ships bigger than whales and travelling far and wide like the men in sharp uniforms, or just to see whales. Would she find the mighty whale from her Piribi's stories if she tried?

Did Yul ever find the great whale?

If he couldn't, how can you, Iro? She scolds herself.

Her dreams are rather simple. But other times, the legends urge her curious mind to simply scour the ocean for the guardians of her grandmother's island. Find Moïco and ask him to turn Old Man Ehri into a slug. Yes, that will do. But what if she finds Myia? Iro would make sure Tebishiro won't have to sell another parcel again on the Big Island.

❖ ❖ ❖

Two legends about Myia make their way to Iro's log:

- Firstly, a giant blue prawn is at the bottom of the Big Island. So Maa-ji says.
- For some reason, Myia sounds more like a lobster than a prawn in Maa-ji's tales. Let's just call him a crustacean. Maa-ji gets easily confused now.
- Myia is dispersed around the island as a million translucent crabs. He will come when called.

— Maa-ji is a horrible storyteller. Now the pig with a fish tail will wake Myia. No crabs are there.

— Ask Maa-ji to tell more about Yul. Yul is the key.

— *Myia is real.*

All she needs to do is follow the lighthouse and find the great blue prawn that lives beneath the island. So she plans her little trip. A trip that results in her getting grounded.

OLD MAN EHRI

Ehri fans himself with an old, yellowing newspaper he has tucked under his arm, and some of its ink has transferred onto his shirt now damp from sweat. He's simply too far from his little honey farm. Drawing another deep sigh for the endless time since his arrival, he scrunches up his nose as he stares down his assistant who is jotting down names of every passenger boarding Old Man Ehri's ferries for the Big Island. He will have to charge them by the end of the month. He's too sour for such an early morning.

Certainly, the chief of the island has better things to do than stand at the pier with his portly belly brushing over the ledger, making his assistant constantly pull his pen back.

Certainly?

But no. Not Old Man Ehri. He needs something to crib about the entire day if he is to get any sleep. Luckily, the prime cause of his anger quietly slips past him with a small round boat on her head, too little to be spotted by him.

Old Man Ehri goes aboard for final inspection of the ferry before it is set to sail. His sharp eyes take in everything. The inspectors on the Big Island did it, why shouldn't he?

Now it's a regular occurrence for the people of Enmei, their tasks delayed by a good half-hour due to their Chief's morning inspection, his glare akin to being smothered by a dozen squids. Old Man Ehri was going above and beyond to appear in the good graces of the new Governor-General who lived in the gabled house on the Big Island. The ones who did often receive good favours, and Ehri were bent on taking his little honey business to the mainland with the Big Officer's help.

The passengers stand wearily, waiting their turn, whining and groaning as Ehri passes them by.

'You do this every day. Can you not give it a rest?' someone says.

He pretends not to hear, moving on to the next luggage, passing Tebishiro, but pulls back, the aroma wafting up from his baskets making Ehri's mouth water. Pulling himself together, Old Man Ehri harrumphs and moves ahead, till he spots something unusual.

A round, upturned boat sits in one corner, failing miserably at trying to appear inconspicuous. With silent steps, Ehri makes his way to the boat, and knocks on top of it. The boat doesn't budge. Sighing, Ehri nudges the boat once again. This time, the little boat lifts off the rough floorboards and scurries away faster than he can catch up.

'Stop that—that—thing! Someone!' Old Man Ehri screams, trying to catch up with the boat that trips up many men on the ferry.

Before anyone can intervene, Ehri gets to it and plops down on the Dongi, proud of himself. 'Now where were you scampering off to? Oye! I'm talking to you!'

A loud mumble comes from beneath Old Man Ehri, followed by a kick that makes the village chief jump up in shock.

The boat turns upside down and out comes Iro, panting

heavily, gulping in the sea air. She lies down flat on the ferry's dirty floor. With one eye closed to shut out the harsh sun, Iro finds Tebishiro gawking at her and sends him an awkward, simpering smile.

'How—Irah?' Tebishiro starts, but Old Man Ehri then clears his throat, raising one bushy brow and lifts her boat up, pulling Iro up as well.

'Off my boat, Tebishiro.'

THE BIG ISLAND

The strong stone pier, a red and white boathouse and jetty were the first things that greeted the people as they docked their boats and ferries while the boatman charged them by the hour. Of course, they would, Tebishiro rues, hefting onto his back the large basket of parcels that he and Cana had prepared in the early hours in Poi's kitchen and carrying it up the slippery steps, shielding his dark eyes from the harsh noon glare. Someone ought to pay for that big gabled house on top of the hill, and it wasn't going to be the uniformed ones.

Tired as he is from all the rowing, the heady fragrance of rice coated in a spicy fish curry makes his mouth water. The sharp, coal-like aroma of the mackerel he had roasted with Iro makes the boatman turn to look at him, eyeing his basket with greedy eyes. The man ought to be hungry as well, standing alone on the pier since the wee hours of the morning. Perhaps when Tebishiro is done with his sale, he will sit down with the boatman and share a meal with him before setting off for home.

He drags his feet along the slippery pier, calculating how much of a loss he has incurred. They'd have no choice but to give away the parcels. The visitors at Poi never really ate much anyway.

Grateful for the grey skies sans a beam of light when he set off, now he squints up at the harsh glare of the sun. *Ask your fireball to be gentler, great god Moïco,* Tebishiro almost whines as a child would in front of a parent. He had set off from Enmei at the crack of dawn in his small boat, prevented from boarding Old Man Ehri's ferries which were five times faster than Tebishiro's, and he couldn't negotiate with him anymore. What prudence is he to expect from someone who picks a fight with an eight-year-old child? *His* eight-year-old?

Sulking, Tebishiro trudges along, standing in line with the others as they go through inspection on the jetty, placing whatever they have brought with them upon a worn but sturdy table. Odette, the Sergeant posted at the jetty, stands by the side, observing everyone with her scrutinizing, sleep-deprived glare, not in the mood to be lax today, the little silver anchors on her red epaulettes glinting gold in the sun. One parcel for her as well, then.

'Snapper?' Odette asks, testing her knowledge as Tebishiro carefully places the basket on the table for inspection.

'Mackerel. Iro helped,' Tebishiro says with a bright smile, his crooked teeth shining against umber skin.

Whenever Tebishiro smiled, a smile so genial and kind—a smile Iro had inherited—it brought a smile to everyone's faces, even those with the harshest of hearts, his mother said. Tebishiro hasn't smiled for a long time now. But he did whenever he talked about Iro.

'Just one basket?' Odette asks.

'Old Man Ehri. Iro boarded the ferry. He found out.'

He needn't explain much. Old Man Ehri did have quite a reputation, even amongst the people here.

'Ah. On your way, then.' Odette gives him a sympathetic smile, stepping out of his way as the soldier nods at her. 'Don't be too late. It seems like it will rain.'

'Thank you Madam,' he beams, straining to pick up the basket. 'I will leave your parcel at the Bakery!' Tebishiro waves at her and goes on his way.

'Bring her around next time!'

❖ ❖ ❖

The Sergeant's rather reserved husband, not much older than Tebishiro, owns a small bakery set up by the foreigners, and it always smells of decadence. The man with sand-like hair came to the island aboard a gleaming ship when Odette got assigned to the island cluster with the rest of their troops. The Sergeant belonged to the mainland, and people had not taken kindly to her marrying one of the outsiders. She cared little for their words and opinions. Instead, the Sergeant chose to start anew on the island when she got the chance. Tebishiro had the chance to meet the newlywed pair when he came scouring for a place to set up his stand for Poi. The baker too, it seemed, had the same idea, looking ponderously at the empty two-room shop, a simple red brick structure with a plain marble floor suitable to both their needs.

Mr Baxter, he is called. Nathaniel Baxter of a small village on the border of his country. He had asked Tebishiro to set up shop with him, an offer Tebishiro had to decline. No one apart from the new islanders had the permission to claim any land, least of all, him. He did, however, agree to set up his stand beneath the bakery's white-and-blue striped canopy. Now no one would question it. It became an arrangement which proved to be mutually beneficial.

The tantalizing aroma and crunch of freshly made loaves of

bread and sweet cinnamon rolls the people from the mainland brought with them waft through the tall, arched windows, as the morning sun casts kaleidoscopic rays upon the marbled floor through the stained glass, beckoning buyers to the shop. These uniformed people loved pairing the scrumptious fresh bread with the spicy roasted fish Tebishiro brought regularly, and asked for more.

Mr Baxter isn't at the counter yet, Tebishiro notices, picking up a large stack of small ceramic plates to keep beside his station. These new islanders didn't like touching the leaf parcels, and would open their twines only once they were served in plates. He starts to set up shop in front of the Bakery, placing a banner that is a riot of colours that Iro had painted—*Poi's*—and unpacks all the food with dexterous hands. First comes the roasted fish and sticky rice wrapped in betel leaves, crunchy wild yam chips only Piribi could make, and then a large glass jar of *Dumla* pickle—bird-lime—its lid covered in linen and secured with twine, a wondrous contradiction of tart and something of earth. Finished, Tebishiro looks out for buyers, avoiding looking around. He couldn't afford to.

The elders say that children barely have any recollection of their early years. But Tebishiro remembers everything about his home. Well, no... he would not say that. It wasn't his island now, and the new inhabitants didn't like reminders of the past, else he would be made to join the ones who were taken to *that* island where the others were. The Dark Place, where the 'rebels' from the mainland were being put to work.

None of his old island remained. In place of round mud huts on strong timber stilts and conical thatched roofs impermeable to rain, there now stood block structures made of brick and concrete, impermeable to the harsh temperament of the great ocean. He remembered his mother drying herbs with the ladies from the village on a sunny day, in the area near the jetty, but now huge cylindrical boilers meant to treat water took their place. A paved path led up the hill and towards the Big Officer's bungalow where there were parties held each month—a gabled house whose timber was taken from the trunk of Yul's parent tree whose root they couldn't reach. The island even got a new name, named after the first big officer who lived in the big gabled house. Wallis Island. Yet, in the precipice of the island, the seascape remains the same, the vast jewel-like ocean from where Enmei appears to be just a blip. The giant myrtle tree in whose shade he had played still stands proudly, burgeoning with pink and purple crumpled parchment-like flowers that fall on the immaculately dressed women talking rather animatedly, undoubtedly the uniformed men's wives who come from the mainland.

No, he wouldn't think of the big gabled house now, nor his old home, Tebishiro shudders. There were many whom he knew had gone into the gabled house and were never seen again. Were they sent to the Dark Place as well, he wouldn't know.

Shaking himself free of these thoughts, he plasters on a big smile and shouts, at once seeing people come up to him. It was going to be a good day. He would make sure of it.

THE DARK PLACE

The sun didn't shine on the Dark Place the way it did on Enmei. Piribi said those who were chosen by Côl, the great god of afterlife, were made to come there, and neither the sun nor the moon could deny the mighty Côl his right.

There are no sand shores, no shining lagoons where one can fish, no hillocks to sit on. Just a rock with a thicket of trees where not even the animals choose to live which merge with the mangroves that spread out to the east of the island. It does have a stone pier—not nearly as sophisticated or sturdy as the one on Wallis Island—where boats from the moored ships arrive with men fettered in chains. The ships, Tebishiro describes, come by each month from the mainland where he says an officer even bigger in post than the Governor-General lives. They bring with them produce, rice, metal, building material meant solely for the Big Island, and packed at the bottom of the vessel. Rebels.

These rebels come in numbers far greater than they can fit on the boats, and then they disappear into the woods.

The Big Officer is making them make a home for themselves, little one, says Piribi whenever Iro asks, *just like how we made Poi. Understood?*

How? Iro doesn't. There is nothing on the island they could make a home with.

❖ ❖ ❖

Some nights, the rebels sing so loud. Songs not cheerful, but full of longing for their homes like Piribi sometimes hums. They sing of a world without chains, and Iro sits on the raised platform of her house as her clattering charms and pendants give music to their songs.

But Piribi and Tebishiro still sit with solemn faces. Cana never goes out. She stays in Poi's kitchen, making preparations for the next day with trembling hands, pretending not to hear the sounds.

And the ocean? It stays silent the entire time. Great god Tarai knows what comes next.

The night after—it always is—the ever-glowing green gaze of the lighthouse on the rebels' island shuts, and like clockwork, polished boats from the Big Island embark for the Dark Place.

Tarai has guests, little one, Piribi says, going to the shore where she sits and prays to Moïco and Tarai for a safe passage over the cane bridge for the rebels.

No songs are heard for a while.

The Big Officer doesn't like it when they sing.

Yet, soon, the songs begin again.

TARAI'S WRATH

'Tarai is snoring again,' Piribi mutters.

Iro immediately perks up, but the old woman keeps her hazy gaze fixed on the roiling dark sky. An unexpected storm has started brewing, replacing the bright sunlight that had been there moments before. 'Or he is furious. Irah?'

'Maa-ji?' Iro asks, jumping down the steps of their restaurant.

'Bring me some of that fig bark, will you? And the Malacca root.'

She doesn't stay to see if Iro followed her words, and is already walking to the shore, kneeling to inspect the stones lying there. The people of Enmei refer to Piribi as the village's wise woman, bearer of ancient secrets known only to her. People come to her to seek solutions for their worries, finding comfort in the quiet manner in which she helps them. Today, she seeks to do the same, but for the sake of her own family.

Iro stands by her side diligently as Cana observes the two, worry etched on her sweet features. Piribi never bothered with needless worries.

Bring Iro's baba home safely, great guardian Myia, Cana prays to the ocean.

Piribi sits on the straw mat, tying together the roots with twine, one little parcel for each stone, while Iro creates a pile of smooth stones. Piribi then lays the stones in two symmetrical lines, creating a path from their home to the brink of water, and gently places the twigs beneath each stone.

All the while, she sings an old folksong—a lullaby for Tarai's sleep to be peaceful. Finished, Piribi stands in the middle of the path, and utters a gentle prayer to Myia and Mite.

Tebishiro must find his way back home.

❖ ❖ ❖

Tebishiro bids Mr Baxter farewell, gathering his baskets before sprinting for the jetty. The road had been closed by the forces while the Governor-General's sleek black Daimler he had brought with him on the shining ship passed by. Governor-General Wallis had decided to hold an impromptu meeting with his officials in the Officer's Club, stirring up frenzy.

The light pitter-patter of rain has been dampening the stone pier when Tebishiro spots his boat tied at the very end where the jellyfish usually gather. *He hadn't left it there.* He is one of the last few fishermen and merchants leaving the Big Island before they close down the jetty, unmooring their boats and ferries as quickly as they can. By the time Tebishiro reaches his boat, the sprinkle turns into a deluge, soaking everything in sight.

He rows and rows through the foaming waves and rising tides that push him against the current and towards the Dark Place. *No, not there...* Tebishiro prays.

The bamboo basket he forgot to tether in a rush to get

back home falls overboard and disappears into the storm. Would anyone know he's stuck in the middle of the ocean? Tebishiro's is the only boat bound for Enmei. His companions for each day had already returned on Old Man Ehri's ferry. It's cold—the sort that never touched their islands, with ice chips hitting Tebishiro, his fingers numbing from the intense chill.

Right behind him, the swirls touch the water. Tebishiro is caught in an intense storm.

'Myia... Tarai... help me go back home. Please help me....' He prays to the roiling dark skies, rowing faster. He can almost make out the outline of the white shore of Enmei, but the storm is swelling up faster.

He can see his home and Poi now, their thatched roofs waving in the strong winds. Tebishiro struggles to paddle over the brink where the calm backwaters meet the choppy waves, but in vain. He begins to lose hope, but a strong current pushes him over the edge and into the safe waters of his lagoon.

Tebishiro sighs loudly, putting his head in his hands. The great god Tarai must have heard him. He ought to have. He sends up a silent prayer as he reaches the shore through pouring rain, stumbling through the path Piribi had laid out. Iro's curious face dashes away from the window as she sprints down the slippery stairs to hug him with all the force she can muster.

But it's not just Tebishiro that the waves push over the brink.

THE SPECTRE

Piribi stands on the shore with her daughter-in-law, a hand over her eyes, and grumbles under her breath. Iro's boat bobs in the calm water in the distance, far enough so that Cana won't be able to catch her, her small legs hanging off the side of her boat's ledge as she languidly sways the small stick with a net attached to the bottom to catch some fish on a lazy day.

Perhaps they should have been clearer when they grounded Iro, but they can't really fault her. The girl earned her leisure.

'I can't leave for the island,' Tebishiro had said as he made his way back to the house, taking out his own small boat he had stowed away for the meantime.

'What happened?' asked Piribi.

He simply waved his hands between Iro and his basket. 'What were you doing, Irah? Do you know how unsafe it is?'

Iro stood silent behind Piribi.

'Okay!' Tebishiro announced. 'No more finding blue prawns or any other thing. No more trips out as well, else your Dongi will

be put in the shed. Understood? And find me a way to finish the parcels. How am I supposed to sell them?'

Tebishiro's old boat was not equipped to handle his weight along with the baskets. Ruefully, he left behind one basket still steaming with delicious food from Poi. But what was he to do? Old Man Ehri had rather haughtily proclaimed Tebishiro would only board his ferry once he had taught Iro some manners. Of course he had walked out on the village chief, furious with the older man for mocking Iro.

Iro regretted boarding the ferry, surrounded by a horde of angry faces, including Tebishiro's. She knew what would happen next. Wasn't she supposed to surprise Tebishiro on the ferry? Sneak out, continue the search, and ask him to pick her back up on his way back home? Turns out, she needed to work on her ideas a little better.

'Irah, Shiro isn't an octopus who will pluck you from the sea and put you back into the ferry!' Piribi admonished her. 'Now finish all this food. You made it, after all.'

'I can't eat all that!'

'Well, too bad, then.'

Iro sent searching glances back and forth between Tebishiro pushing his boat into the water and the basket.

Finish the parcels.

❖ ❖ ❖

Iro is used to the stares of the villagers whenever she travels. Who wouldn't, if they saw her land-boat? Now was no time for the scenic route, she mouths to herself as she hurries down the main road and onto the pier. She stops in front of the sweets vendor who sits with a sour face, swatting flies away from his confectionaries.

'Oye barfi wale uncle!' she calls out, heaving the heavy basket, its woven design drawing patterns in the sand. *What was his name?* Iro doesn't remember. But she knows he mixes stale batches with his new ones.

The old man looks down at her, stunned by her outspoken behaviour but more so embarrassed at being laughed at by passers-by. '*Oye barfi wale?* Tebishiro's girl, aren't you? I've seen you around.'

She nods defiantly. Iro doesn't stumble. Instead, she sizes up Old Man Bilik and stands a little straighter. 'Poi's special roasted mackerel and rice. A hundred parcels. My Maa-ji made it this morning.' She points at the basket, beaming with pride. 'Sell it.'

The man's sparse eyebrows shoot up into his receding hairline. 'And why would I do that?'

'Okay. I can take this to the chief,' she replies nonchalantly, and begins to retreat.

Now the reason why she had chosen the sweets seller was, the old man had an ongoing feud with Old Man Ehri. Over a play for the festival. A whole raffle had taken place and the villagers voted between him and Old Man Ehri to play Myia. But who could vote against Old Man Ehri? Only so much could escape Iro's ears, and the visitors at Poi weren't the quiet sort either.

'Wait, girl!' Old Man Bilik calls out, eyeing the large basket. Oh, what a profit it would turn in! 'Tebishiro didn't take it?'

'He had a fight with Old Man Ehri. He stopped Baba from boarding the ferry.' Iro frowns. 'You can sell them here, and I will let you keep half the profit.'

No need to tell him the rest.

'Why not sell them yourself?'

'I'm eight. Will you buy from an eight-year-old?'

Old Man Bilik mulls over her proposal, eyeing the basket. Splitting profit wouldn't hurt. 'I will sell them. What's the price Tebishiro sells it for?'

'*Duanni* for rice, *athanni* for fish,' she lies nimbly. 'One rupee for both.'

Two anna for rice, eight anna for fish? Outrageous.

'Throw in the rabbits, and you have a deal,' Old Man Bilik gruffly says, pointing to the fluffy civets. 'No one would buy them for that much.'

'They are not rabbits.'

'Will still make a tasty stew,' he argues, eyeing them.

'The people on the Big Island always buy for that much,' Iro replies, standing in front of Beyan and Koio.

'You aren't on the Big Island now, are you?'

'See, I thought you won't be able to afford it. I should have gone to the chief.'

'Wait!' he calls out. If it sells, he will make more profit in a day than he could selling sweets all summer. It couldn't hurt. 'I'll buy it. But first, whom did your Ma-Baba pick for the play?'

A play? He is still sour over losing his lead role to Old Man Ehri?

'You, Uncle.' Iro smiles, pushing the basket forward.

'You have a deal, then. Let's sell your Poi's—'

'*You* sell them,' Iro interrupts. 'I have work.'

'You're eight. What work could you have?' he asks.

But Iro doesn't stay. She is already fixing her hat back and turning her land-boat around for Poi. 'Half the profit. Deal.'

❖ ❖ ❖

By noon, Old Man Bilik stands outside Iro's house and hands over the profit—half of the total amount—to Cana, along with two sacks of rice. Cana is stunned, but takes it regardless.

'This girl...' Piribi says, clicking her tongue. 'She made a profit. More than Shiro could in a month.'

'At triple cost, Amma. She is hustling old people!' Cana shakes her head in disbelief. She reaches the edge of the sand, ready to scold Iro. 'Irah! Come back!'

Iro sits up straight and peeks over the edge of the boat like an owlet.

'I'm telling you, Cana, let this girl handle your business and soon she won't need to work a day in her life!' Piribi chortles, going back inside with Cana following her closely.

❖ ❖ ❖

Iro drags her small oar out to make her way back, and starts pulling in her net, but is met with resistance.

She tugs it again, but the net tugs back harder.

The water is clear enough in the lagoon, but Iro sits in the deeper waters, making it harder to see. Just then, Iro feels a little wave pass right below her boat, as though a large fish just passed her by. The water is calm again. Could it be Myia? A mermaid? Or something worse? *Think, Iro. What could be hiding here?*

She feels the wave again, followed by a soft bump at the bottom of her boat. Something is definitely there. Iro paddles away faster, getting out of the water as quickly as she can to where Cana is winnowing rice on a bamboo mat, husking the small, pearly grains while Piribi sits a little away, weaving together another basket for Tebishiro to carry to the Big Island.

'Irah—there's food here!' Cana exclaims, brushing off the sand Iro has dragged with her in a rush to reach her.

'Ma, I think Myia just passed below my boat.' Iro falls down beside Cana, sticking the husks in her white hair.

'Myia is a lot bigger than your boat, Irah...' Cana ruffles her daughter's short curls, chuckling as she carries on her daily chores. 'Were you hiding in your Dongi?'

'...yes?'

'You cannot just hide in boats like that. Or make deals behind our backs. What if someone took advantage of that?'

'I know,' Iro says nonchalantly, sitting on the floor with her legs splayed out, crossing and uncrossing her big toes, making a play of it. 'You should have seen me, Ma! Old Man Bilik made big eyes and said *"half the profit is yours!"*'

Cana can't hold back any longer and dissolves in a fit of laughter.

❖ ❖ ❖

If only it were a little brighter, Iro wishes, walking around her mother to go outside. Slowly, she climbs down the bamboo stairs, trying to maintain her balance. The halloos of scops owls from the nearby woods urge the macaques to howl in the middle of night, spooking her, but Iro braves on. Occasionally, she would hear the guttural croak of bullfrogs. Now those scared her, yet she doesn't falter in her steps.

Much like every house on Enmei, her house too has the restroom and bath standing a little further away from the main house. The owls hoot again, and Iro starts climbing the ladder back up. She can wait till Piribi is up. Can she?

Go back? Or not? Iro muses. *Ha! Go back and be called a bedwetter again? No!*

Kicking up white sand still a little warm from the harsh sun, she slowly makes her way to the restroom, fear dampened by urgency. But a little silhouette upon the rock captures her attention, and Iro freezes.

Just in front of her, something lies on the smooth rock, still and blinking at her. She can see the beady eyes and the head full of long unruly curls bobbing in her direction.

It can't be. Can it? Her mind is coming up with all possibilities, rare and common. A ghost? A sea siren, what is it? But then the thing tilts its head, and Iro lets out a terrified scream, making the silhouette flinch. She runs back inside and burrows herself in her mother's side, shaking like a leaf.

'Irah?' Cana groggily asks, hugging her tighter. 'What happened?'

Should she tell her family? Or wait?

'...a bullfrog. It jumped at me and I got scared,' Iro lies. No, she won't tell a soul till she confirms what exactly the creature is. From all the fables she's heard, she is certain it's a mermaid.

But soon, a bright smile lights up her tiny face. Myia had brought a magical mermaid to her lagoon, and if she is in her lagoon, that means she can capture her and make her do magic. Magic that can help her get even with Old Man Ehri.

❖ ❖ ❖

Iro's *spectre* sits by the rocks, not so much drowsy as exhausted, and looks at the little girl with hair like clouds staring in her direction with her mouth hanging open. She doesn't think much of it. What can the girl see in the dark?

But then the girl lets out a shrill scream and stumbles all the way back to the house.

The girl's scream startles her, and she retreats into the dark water, munching on the tufts of sea grass that had gathered on her head as she had come up from beneath the water's surface. She sputters, spitting out the rancid-tasting browning plant, and paddles over the water with her flippers as gently as she can.

She will come back when the loud girl isn't there. But something tells her this isn't the last she had seen of the pesky white-haired girl on the beach.

A WOODPECKER'S HOLLOW

There weren't many people who lived in Enmei, and everyone knew everyone. But twenty-two years ago, people from nearby islands started arriving in small boats, carrying whatever little belongings they had. Their empty faces held a haunted look, and the natives of Enmei knew. They knew. And wished they weren't next. But Enmei held no charm for the Big Officer, and they were spared.

All settled in now, Old Man Ehri, doing his duty as the village chief, brought with him a jar of his homemade honey, and sat Cana and Tebishiro down to convince them to start a small business. They didn't know what to do. Most of Enmei's produce had already been taken to the Big Island to feed the workers and soldiers, and they didn't know whether the meagre catch of fish from their small lagoon would suffice.

'You can cook, can you not?' Piribi chided them, supporting Old Man Ehri. 'Do you think someone who has toiled the entire day in heat would want raw produce? They need something to eat right away. Feed them.'

It took Tebishiro weeks to get a small structure made by their hut—identical, but with a cooking and preparing area.

Soon, word spread and more people came to visit, curious. They loved the food and paid them well for it.

Could it be? Could their venture really just start like this? The pair did wonder how to proceed, what to call themselves, but then Iro uttered her very first word, pointing to a bird. Piribi, however, told a different story.

'You have a child who runs into trees, Shiro,' Piribi had said, wrapping a cold cloth around Iro's head as the two-year-old screamed, *let's just call her Poi.*

I can't call her a woodpecker, Amma.

She behaves like one.

But the name stuck. *Poi*—woodpecker's hollow—a small lunch service with a sitting area where customers sat outside, bringing their own mats, enjoying their meals and the calm waters of the lagoon. With enough money saved, Tebishiro bought more rice and spices and started taking his baskets up to the Big Island, boarding Old Man Ehri's ferries.

It was a setup that had saved them, and started a tradition of each season's jar of honey to be gifted to Piribi.

❖ ❖ ❖

Iro tries to put together the words in the thin colourful book that Tebishiro had brought home a few days ago, trying to make sense of it. He had bought a new set of linen shorts and loose half-sleeved cotton shirt, like the ones Iro normally wore, but these were a pristine white.

He had made a profit and bought gifts for everyone but himself.

'The children in the barracks too wear this!' he had said proudly, watching with joy as Iro marvelled at the shiny clothes. But it wasn't enough.

Tebishiro reached into his bag and took out a parcel wrapped in old yellowing newspaper and twine and handed it over to Iro. She carefully unwrapped it to reveal a pair of shiny brown leather sandals. Iro was certain no one in all of Enmei would have something so pretty. Oh, how majestic she would look walking into the island! Even Old Man Ehri would not have anything to say, jealous as he would be of her.

Iro had been lost in her musings when Tebishiro revealed the most wonderful gift of all, a gift chosen by Odette and her baker husband. In Iro's small hands, he placed a thin black slate, a box of chalks of which two sticks he had accidentally broken, and a slim book with unfamiliar letters. The Sergeant herself had visited the one-room school by the barracks and asked the teacher for an elementary book for a beloved child, and the kind old man had happily complied.

Tebishiro now sat with Mr Baxter for an hour longer after all their sales were done. Mr Baxter taught him alphabets and word formation, which he, in turn, would teach Iro. Iro was proud to admit that, during her little lessons, she had made her Ma and grandmother learn a little as well. But at the moment, she could barely focus on her task, lost as she was in her thoughts about the mermaid.

Yes, Iro is daydreaming. What beautiful hair the mermaid must have, of a really bright opal like the iridescent shells that usually washed ashore. Her fin must be bright as well. But what if the tales of the mermaid weren't true, Iro gasps, scared of her own thoughts. What if she was really half-fish, half-woman, but the other way around? Or worse still, not a mermaid at all, but a water wraith!

Iro shudders at the thought. Soon, she will find out. All she needs is the tide and Dongi by her side.

❖ ❖ ❖

Iro busies herself with her books, trying to look calm. But then she sees her Ma leave the room with her jute basket. This is it. This is her chance.

'Maa-ji?' she calls out to Piribi. 'What did Yul look like?'

Piribi looks at her granddaughter, taking in the docile expression on her face. She is up to something, she knows. 'Why?'

'I just wanted to know what he looked like. What if he looked like a bird? What if he looked like us, but his face was all feathery?'

'Then he looked like a bird.' Piribi shrugs, returning to her basket.

'Can other things be like that too? Like a fish?'

'That would be the pig in the water. I told you about that one, didn't I?' Piribi carries on, already lost in her story. 'Yul once got hungry and chased a pig across the island. Now this pig was faster than anything, and it ran to the edge of the island's cliff. It saw Yul run behind him and it jumped into the water. Yul threw a giant kobo leaf at it. Once the pig touched the water, its limbs dissolved and the leaf became its tail.'

'Not a pig, Maa-ji! But a woman with long hair and a fish-like tail.'

'Ah. That's a mermaid. I told you about them too.' Piribi slowly starts to get up, placing one hand on the ground to ease the pain in her knees. 'They used to come with the seafoam and play on the shores.'

'Do these mermaids swim very fast?' Iro asks, following her outside Poi.

'Uh-huh...'

'Do they sit on rocks?'

'Yes.'

'Maa-ji, we have a mermaid in our lagoon!' Iro blurts out.

Piribi slips on the final rung of the ladder and falls on her back in the sand.

'Maa-ji!'

'What?' Piribi croaks, wincing in pain, slowly sitting up with Iro's help. She had not expected that.

'We have a mermaid, Maa-ji. In the water.'

'Our water? This lagoon?'

Iro nods furiously.

'Are you sure?' This is it, Piribi thinks with dread. All the times her granddaughter had hit her head had finally caught up with her. Or perhaps the creatures were real after all... Were they?

'Very,' Iro says with confidence. 'I saw her sitting by the rocks at night, and now I'm going to catch her.'

CANARDS OF A MERMAID

It starts off as a whisper, gradually transforming into a murmur that echoes in almost every other house in Enmei, with everyone trying to keep it a secret. A mermaid has called the calm waters of their little island home and they all want to have her for themselves. She would bring them unbelievable riches, if the fables were to be believed.

You see what happened is, Piribi and Old Man Bilik struck an accord, seeing the profit they had made together. Cana and Tebishiro would still prepare two baskets of food, with one going to the Big Island, and another with him at the small pier. Most islanders would leave on the boats and ferries with the first light, and they needed a packed lunch. Perhaps Iro had talked up the rates a little much, but it was still pittance in comparison to the food sold on the Big Island, and the buyers were happy to pay.

In the evening, Old Man Bilik came by to give Cana her share of the profits of the day, but not seeing her anywhere, he walked up to Poi, and saw Piribi take a tumble from the stairs. He rushed to help her up, but saw Iro jump down and make her grandmother sit up. That is when he heard it.

We have a mermaid in our lagoon, Maa-ji... I'm going to catch it.

The little girl's shocking declaration had him retracting and rushing back to his house. Shaking, he recounted every detail to his wife. Enmei was too small an island, where a mere wisp of a whisper in one house would echo in another and make for really interesting gossip. So all it takes is Old Man Bilik's wife to exclaim with joy, and by morning, the houses on the south side knew of the mermaid.

Wouldn't it be wonderful, to have the lost treasures of the ocean in one's hand, or simply to hold a mermaid's tear in one's palm? They were known to be magical, sometimes turning into diamonds, sometimes pearls, and sometimes, the most coveted of all, immortality...

Perhaps it's fortunate that the *mermaid* had stumbled into the hands of someone who cared for neither precious gems nor immortality, but only to see Old Man Ehri be turned into a slug.

THE CHILDREN OF CÔL

None knew how the very first of the gods were created, but the ancestors said these divine, powerful, sometimes shallow beings lived within the great ocean for as long as the earth had been there.

The great Côl, mighty god of the afterlife burdened with the weight of the souls, grew overwhelmed with all the lives lost in the petty wars fought among the gods in their bid to lay claim to any and every land. So he created creatures—Ferriers of the land and the sea—to accompany souls on their way to him. But he faced another dilemma. Where would his creations live? So Côl sought an audience with the gods. But none apart from the mighty Moïco answered.

I seek a home for my children, great god Moïco.

But where shall they even live, great Côl? Moïco, the gentle god of fire asked, concerned with the omens of death. *Wouldn't these beings scare the people if they are seen?*

You misunderstand, great Moïco, assured Côl, *just as you have tasked a part of your soul to grace the skies and bring life, I have done the same. This land will flourish, but with it will come great loss as well. I can't be around to bring each soul to the cane bridge, but my children can. Give them a place on the land and the ocean, I urge you.*

As you worry about your children, I do for mine. As would the god of water Tarai. I ask that you adapt your creations. Give them wings like the birds of the north skies who perch upon strong branches of old trees; give them fins and flippers like Tarai's deep ocean creatures who feed upon sea-grass and shells. Let your children be inconspicuous, great Côl, so they may not alarm anyone. You do that, and I assure you your Ferriers shall forever be held in high regard.

Côl mulled over Moïco's words, and finally agreed.

The Ferriers of the sky—he sent them as long-tailed inky birds who swarm the skies in battles. The Ferriers of the ocean—he sent to live beneath islands that witnessed the most loss, the entire host of creatures swimming across the ocean to complete their tasks.

Yet, the loss in the archipelago urged them to stay. For a while they lived beneath the root of the Jarul tree as it was whittled, mourning the loss of the Life Tree as they ferried each life over the bridge. But for many, many years now, the clan lives beneath the Dark Place. Great god Côl had been right, after all.

And sometimes, the Ferriers see a gigantic fanned tail dotted with seashells swiftly dig through the sea bed and disappear in the crevices as the clan lazes at the bottom of the ocean. Myia lives in hiding, disappointed, yet always on a lookout for the voices of the children of Yul as he had sworn to. Would he ever return?

THE FIRST MEET

Curiosity gets the better of Iro's neighbours as they try to sneak up to the lagoon, but none can cross the boundary of Poi. Why, you ask? In order to capture the mermaid, Iro stands guard around the boundary of the beach with a large stick in her hand. Three of the neighbours have already gone back home with bruised ankles, complaining to her parents as they wince in pain. But they couldn't really tell anyone of it now, could they?

'We just came by to catch some fish,' they complained to her grandmother, grimacing in pain. 'You cannot monopolize an entire beach, Amma. Your girl nearly broke my ankle!'

Piribi had looked at the man's ankle with a sour face. Not a bruise in sight, she thought to herself and shooed them away, mumbling to herself as she wove another basket. With the profit they were making behind Tebishiro's back, they needed more leaves for parcels and more baskets to deliver. Iro had even found two more civets to pull her makeshift cart, and their delivery service grew beyond what they had imagined.

They would have to let him know soon enough.

❖ ❖ ❖

Come night, Iro wanders back to the lagoon where she had first seen her mermaid. Five nights, the resolute little girl sat in wait, and five nights there wasn't even a ripple in the water. But on the sixth night, she finally sees movement.

The mermaid emerges from the water, but this time, her long coiled hair is gone.

Odd. Firmly holding her trusted bamboo stick in her tawny hand, Iro casually strolls to the beach, trying not to alert the creature resting near the cluster of rocks.

This time, she had it all sorted out: whack the mermaid on her head and drag her to the house by her tail. Yes, that will do. She had dragged fish the size of her own body countless times with her Baba, how hard could a mermaid be? She needed the courage of Mite by her side right now, undertaking such a huge task alone. Her Ma would not let her dip a toe in water for the rest of her life if she got to know.

She tries to keep her movements calm, as though approaching a small animal, mindful not to look directly at the mermaid. She hums a lullaby her Maa-ji sings to her so many times, and goes to sit on the beach.

It's dark and no one's around, not her Ma and Baba sleeping soundly and her Maa-ji making sure they didn't leave, but Iro, in that moment, feels braver than she has ever been. Myia and Mite had her back. Her Maa-ji had said that they did, and so she believed. If the mermaid did, in fact, drag her into the water, the great blue prawn would come to rescue her.

She doesn't know how long she sits together with the mermaid in silence, but soon, the mermaid's form starts to droop on the rocks. She's getting sleepy. This is it. This was what Iro was waiting for.

As silently as she can, Iro starts to walk towards the rocks, a rough jute rope gripped firmly in her hands, held in hiding behind her back. Tonight would be the night she gets herself a mermaid. Take that, Old Man Ehri.

Iro can see the shape of it rather clearly now. The mermaid looks less of a beautiful woman from where she stands; rather, just a really lumpy fish the size of Iro. Was it even a mermaid, or were the ancestors messing with her right now?

It mattered not, she decides as the form suddenly stirs, coming to its senses, and starts retreating into the dark waters.

Alarmed, Iro sprints as fast as her little feet can carry her to the rocks, only to have the mermaid slip away and disappear into the lagoon.

❖ ❖ ❖

The creature is tired, sleepy, and really, really hungry. The lagoon only had a meagre amount of kelp after days of feasting on them, and she couldn't eat the small fish. Some had taken to sticking by her side, sensing no danger from her. But most importantly, she missed her mother. The strong waves had pushed her over the waves from the safety of her dark island and into the cloud-haired girl's lagoon. Many times she had tried to cross over, but the current kept pushing her back. And now there was this girl, with her stick and constant vigilance of the water.

She swam back lazily, tired, but proud of herself for having shaken the odd girl off. Suddenly, she feels some movement right over her. There's just a faint, blurred yellow light above the water, and then something jumps in and catches her tail.

❖ ❖ ❖

'Got you!' Iro screams, her smile disappearing as she sees

the *mermaid*. But before Iro can react, the *thing* pulls her underwater.

Curses! The weird potato mermaid drags Iro further towards the shallow ocean bed and through the bright corals and translucent sea grass in a bid to be rid of her. Iro catches a mouthful of sand as the creature burrows through the seabed, violently shaking her tail to shake off the grip little Iro has on her.

With one strong whip, the creature is free, and swims off faster than Iro can see.

❖ ❖ ❖

Tired, Iro swims to the surface, familiar with every inch of the lagoon, and makes her way back to her boat. Her face and hands hurt, she is sure she sports more bruises from being knocked into the corals.

Great, she paddles angrily to the shore, her little lamp's flame fluttering slightly in the gentle ocean's breeze. Not only did she not catch a mermaid, her *mermaid* turned out to be a sentient sweet potato.

Mino. That is what she was going to call that monstrosity in the water who had, as of tonight, found an enemy in Iro.

THE FERRIER OF THE OCEAN

A frown had been her constant companion ever since Iro had come face to face with the creature in her lagoon. No, it certainly wasn't a mermaid. What she had found instead was a round, plush looking thing with a flipper and a smooth trunk. Its tiny beady eyes had looked shocked when she had caught its tail.

She had been ready, with her Dongi and a lamp attached on a rod on standby, if she needed to follow the mermaid into the water. The moment the mermaid started retreating, Iro veered in the direction of her boat and paddled, keeping track of the ripple in the water. The mermaid was slow, too slow. But this creature was neither a mermaid, nor possessed any shred of magic.

Now what was she supposed to do?

'Did you find it, then?' Piribi asks in a hushed tone, nudging her. She sat beside Iro, cutting up small bamboo shoots. The girl nods at her before groaning loudly and splaying on the floor, grumbling under her breath.

'What?' Piribi asks.

'It wasn't a mermaid, Maa-ji. It was a...something that looked like a potato,' she replies, puffing her plush cheeks even more.

'Potato?' Piribi asks, blinking. 'Did it have a small trunk, small eyes, a scalloped tail?'

'It was dark, Maa-ji. I couldn't see that much. But it looked like that.'

'Ah...so you did find one of them.'

'Them?' Iro pipes up, curious. 'Not the pig in the water!'

'Them, little moonchild.' Piribi smiles at her, her voice turning rather low as though she's sharing an ancient secret. 'The very last of mermaids.'

'It was round.'

'Just because it was round, it couldn't be a mermaid? What have these people been teaching you?' Piribi clicks her tongue, and gets up to leave.

'Maa-ji!' Iro runs after her. Her grandmother is surprisingly fast for someone who is always complaining about her knees giving her trouble.

'Was it a mermaid, then?' Iro persists.

'The same magic that steeps through everything in our island runs through the creatures in it as well, little one. You remember the tale of our first ancestor, don't you? How did all the creatures in the skies and waters come to protect him so he could grow? The creature that is in our waters is one of those same creatures. They are gentle, pure souls, bringing fortune wherever they go, a true mermaid—Ferriers of the ocean created by the great god of afterlife—and it is our duty to protect them as their ancestors did for ours. These creatures guide our dead to the afterlife, little one. It's their task to take them to the cane bridge.'

'But doesn't Tarai walk with them?'

'Only the bravest are fortunate to have the great god of the ocean guide them, Irah. He provides them a safe passage to the bridge. But only to those who aren't wicked. Find the creature. She shouldn't be here.'

Wide-eyed, Iro listens intently to her grandmother, and off she goes to the shore to find the sea creature she had lost.

❖ ❖ ❖

'Mino!' Iro screams to the empty calm ocean, sitting cross-legged on the small strip of beach. 'I have to protect you! My Maa-ji said so!'

It was an apt name for the creature—no, true mermaid. Even if she looks like a potato. But wouldn't the creature be offended if it got to know? Mino it was going to be.

She sits tearing small strips of browning sea grass washed ashore, squinting her dark eyes to observe the calm lagoon for any movement. The water is beginning to rise and soon the lagoon will be full again. Another wave rolls in, tangling more sea grass around Iro's feet, and with it brings more of the small translucent crabs that scramble to get away from her.

'Yuck!' She careens, trying to remove the slimy leaves from her toes, but her fingers are still. *Sea grass*. It wasn't hair on the creature's head. She knew just how to draw her mermaid out, as smelly as it may be.

❖ ❖ ❖

By evening, Iro had collected a rather huge, stinking pile of sea grass, and was busy strewing it around the coastline. It wasn't perhaps the best-laid of plans, but who was going to tell her?

'What are you doing?' Cana asks, coming up behind her. She scrunches her nose at the small mounds that now dot the beach.

'Laying bait,' she replies briskly, not stopping in her task. 'I have a debt to repay.'

Cana gapes at her. This child sometimes stuns her. 'What debt? Do we owe Old Man Bilik money?'

'No...'

'Then?'

'It's between me and the sea.'

'Well, did the sea tell you to gather all this? It's rotten, Irah. At least use fresh ones that can be used later. Oye!' Cana calls out, toeing the now drying grass, Iro having travelled quite a distance from where Cana stands.

'Maa-ji did!'

Cana simply gawks at her daughter. There was no telling what Iro would do till she had done it, and she would rather not interfere with the duo. 'Well, don't take too long!'

'I won't!'

❖ ❖ ❖

Five more minutes, Iro tells herself, tired of waiting. It had been hours, and now she's getting hungry. The sky is beginning to turn purple, and her father will soon be back from the Big Island. Just five more minutes, and if the mermaid doesn't show up, I'm going to call it off.

Luring true mermaids was harder than it looked.

❖ ❖ ❖

Her five minutes turn into half an hour, and Iro is exhausted. And hungry. Sighing, she gets up, dragging her small feet through the sand still hot to touch.

And then, she finally hears it—little plops in the water, distinct from the calm ocean farther away. A small head rises a little above the surface, curiously peeking, and goes back in. Startled, Iro runs to hide behind Poi's stairs, watching with interest. The creature pops its head back over the water, this time closer. It continues so for a while, resurfacing, then slithering back into hiding till it is nearly at the rocks. The thing pokes its head around the wilted sea grass Iro had put there, and recoils in disgust before going back into the water.

'Argh!' Iro screams, stomping her feet in the sand. All her efforts dragging the stinking pile had been for nothing. The creature hates it.

But she hears the plop again, and this time, it's accompanied by a shallow whistle-like sound, quite like the ones she had heard in the distance from whales. Shocked, Iro stands by the rocks, and sees the creature get closer and closer to her. Now, she can see it clearly.

The creature is small, not much larger than she. It doesn't have opalescent scales like she saw on the fish, but wrinkled skin that looks like the lilac paint her Ma made from crushing those pearly shells, a scalloped tail, and small, shiny, pitch-black eyes. It swims using its paddle-like flippers. The creature is as slow over the surface as fast it was under the water. She has no idea whether it is fully-grown or just a calf, but it looks so small that she wants to reach out and touch it. *Be careful, Iro, she warns herself, even as a calf, this thing almost upset your boat.*

The creature carries something in its mouth, and drops it by the wet sand before retreating to its regular spot by the rocks, looking expectantly at Iro. Was it shy? Seeing Iro not move, the creature whistles again, as if it were whining.

Iro quickly glances around to make sure her Ma and grandma are nowhere in sight, and takes hesitant steps. Slowly, she pokes the little lump with a stick to see if it moves.

Seeing no response, she picks it up, pinching it between her small fingers.

It's a wad of translucent, bright green sea grass freshly pulled from the ocean bed. Neither is it wilted, nor stinking.

Oh.

Iro flushes, red creeping up her neck and heating her ears. The true mermaid keeps looking at her expectantly as she pick up the sea grass and walks towards the rocks, placing the small pile in front of the creature. This time, the true mermaid reaches out and eats it.

Iro giggles, seeing the enthusiastic little creature noisily munching on the crisp sea grass.

'True mermaid, I am Iro.' She introduces herself with all the formality she can muster. It was a fabled creature from her Maa-ji's island, after all. 'You made me wait too much, but it's okay, and I also know you cannot do magic. Don't worry, though. I won't tell anyone. Can you talk?'

The creature blinks at her and goes back to eating the sea grass.

'I tried!' Iro says aloud to herself, exasperated. 'You are just a small, round pig mermaid, but you're my mermaid. I will call you Mino. Do you like it?'

Iro stretches out her small hand, keeping it in the creature's vision, lest she accidentally spook it, and waits. There is a long silence on both sides, then astonishingly, the creature reaches out, and with its large nose, pats her hand and shyly goes back into the water. She stands in wonder and amazement. Not only had Iro found the true mermaid of her Maa-ji's island but, surprisingly, she had even befriended it.

Well, somewhat befriended it.

TEBISHIRO

It became a routine of sorts for Iro, taking her Dongi out into the middle of the reef and just waiting. She could see how her Mino managed to remain unseen in the clear waters of her lagoon. The creature was tinged the very shade of the rocks beneath, and not much bigger than the fish that swam in it. Iro would try to see, search for her true mermaid, find nothing at first, and suddenly there would be a nudge below her boat, and there it would be.

She didn't have to worry about someone spotting Mino either. Diligently, Iro stood guard around the boundary of the beach with her now feared stick in her hand. None would dare to steal her Mino. She had made it rather clear as she started making a wall around the stones, taking her trusted stick and books with her onto the mat outside, sitting in the shade of her house, and wryly observing the water for any movement.

❖ ❖ ❖

As Moïco's fireball gives way for Tuya to shine, Cana, Piribi and Iro sit on the steps of Poi, waiting for Tebishiro to come trudging down the familiar pathway, carrying a hopefully empty basket and a pocket full of coins. He always had a little upturn of lips—not quite a smile, yet not so weighed down—whenever he could hear the coins jingling in his pocket.

Soon, they hear the familiar trudge—one step lighter, two steps heavier—of Tebishiro walking with a skip in his step that said that he had had a tiring but good day.

Tebishiro steps back, startled by his family looking at him like the owls in the woods did, wide-eyed and scrutinizing, each taking up a rung on the stairs with Iro between them. 'Irah?'

'We were just waiting for you,' Iro grins, a low whistle coming through the empty space where her teeth were yet to grow. 'I'm hungry.'

She jumps off the side and runs to her house, waiting to wash her hands and face by the bowl with her father. They wash in silence, but Tebishiro is alert, wryly observing his daughter. It was time. He leads her gently by the arm and makes her sit with him on the mat, shushing her when she tries to question.

'Amma, Cana, sit down please.'

Tebishiro sits Cana and Piribi down on either side of him, reaching his trousers' back pocket and pulls out a little sack and places it between their dinner bowls. Iro looks stunned, while Piribi merely harrumphs and goes back to eating her meal, unbothered by her son's querying gaze.

'I was sitting in the Bakery with Mr Baxter for lunch, and Old Man Bilik visited. He wished to buy something—I don't know. But then he gave me this. Said it was yesterday's share he couldn't bring around.' He finishes, looking expectantly at his family.

'Now, either he has grown really generous, or you people have done something.'

Sensing the refusal from both Cana and Iro, Piribi sighs, putting down her wooden bowl.

'Old Man Bilik is a partner in trade. Your clever little girl took the basket you had to leave behind and sold it to him for equal profit. In one week, she made the kind of money that the delivery service would take months to.' Piribi sees her son's eyebrows vanish in his dark hair.

'...partner?'

'You did say—"Find a way to finish them!"' Piribi admonishes him. 'Be thankful. You have something to eat, that too when all your food is going towards feeding *them.*'

'Wait...' Tebishiro shakes his head, 'How much? How did you make profit? Irah?'

'Easy.' Iro shrugs. 'I told him I would sell it all to Old Man Ehri. He couldn't wait to buy it after that.'

Tebishiro looks between Piribi and Cana, his mouth hanging open. 'How *much* did you make?'

'Half profit plus two sacks of rice. Every day. For a hundred parcels. She made a deal of *athanni* for fish and *duanni* for rice,' Cana replies.

Tebishiro has to abandon his food and lie down, covering his eyes, overwhelmed. 'Irah?'

Iro hesitantly looks at him, twiddling her fingers.

'Would you like to come with me to the Bakery? Meet Madam Sergeant and Mr Baxter?' Tebishiro asks Iro with a gentle, sorrowful smile that only Cana sees through.

'The Big Island?' Iro asks, wide-eyed.

'Shiro.' Piribi intervenes, her lips set in a grim line.

'The Big Island. Madam Sergeant would love to meet you. Wear your new sandals, okay?' Tebishiro says, walking out of their house as Iro twirls around a just as sorrowful Cana, swinging dangerously close to the bowl of fish curry.

❖ ❖ ❖

'I am proud of her, Amma. Don't doubt that,' Tebishiro says gently to Piribi. 'Madam Sergeant and her husband, they've been kind enough to lend her books. She has offered to talk to the headmaster of the school over there. It isn't much, but the children of the soldiers in barracks attend it as well. She wouldn't be alone.'

His mother had followed him outside, coming to sit in the warm sand beside him. Their lagoon isn't as dark as the rest of Enmei. The lighthouse lights the lagoon like emeralds and the sand still glows white even without the moon in the sky. *Tuya* must be resting.

Rest, mother goddess, and watch over my Iro, Piribi prays.

'Do you really want for her to go learn with them, Shiro? What if they don't allow her?' *They didn't let Tebishiro. Why would they for Iro.*

'A lot has changed. Children from nearby islands attend as well. This is no life for a child, Amma. Enmei isn't a big place. All the children here older than Iro are working on their docks and buildings, and the younger ones are kept hidden in their houses, as though some force is going to come and snatch them. She needs to be around her peers. Amma... she needs to live a full life, and not struggle every moment like we do,' Tebishiro adds, as the green light from the lighthouse begins to dim, gently casting the ocean in darkness.

The Dark Place.

The Big Officer didn't wish for his people to see when the rebels were *sent to the sea.*

Piribi gets up, walks up to the shoreline and kneels down with a heavy heart as Tebishiro looks on, kneeling with her and touching his forehead to the water in prayer.

'Great god Tarai, guide them over the cane bridge as you do for all,' Piribi prays. 'May the great Côl greet them at the gates of afterlife and bless them.'

Would it always be this way? Keep waiting till they are all sent to the Dark Place? Piribi cannot let Iro be one of them. Piribi sits there with a grim face, but relents. Her granddaughter was going to the Big Island.

VISIT TO THE BAKERY

Robust. That is the only word Iro can think of as she steps off the ferry and onto the stone pier with her father, the intimidating red and white jetty in front of her looking all too foreign. Unfamiliar, she sticks to Tebishiro's side, walking hesitantly to join the line.

A little away from them, a boy no older than Iro, sits by the pier holding a basket while another boy swims out to the edge and throws shining black stars into their little basket. Stars in the ocean? Her lagoon held no stars, only sea grass and shells for Mino to munch on.

Curious, Iro kneels to look below the pier while Tebishiro maintains a grip on her sleeve. Surely, the entire stone edge is dotted in black spiney stars and slimy algae creeping upon the pier from the sides like tentacles.

'Baba, there's stars in the water!' she says, already reaching out for them.

'Irah—don't touch them! Tebishiro exclaims, pulling her back up. 'You didn't, right?'

'It's too far down.'

'Good. Now please stay by my side. No more running off,' Tebishiro warns, 'and no more dirtying the uniform. You will have to wash it every day.'

Today, Iro has on her finest clothes, wearing the half-sleeved green cotton shirt she had folded neatly and put beneath her bedding the night before to smooth out the creases. Her hands are balled into fists and stuffed inside the pockets of her navy shorts. She had carefully unpacked the new leather sandals Tebishiro had bought for her, marvelling at their shine before putting them on.

Piribi had grumbled under her breath the entire time Iro was getting ready, but still made sure she was scrubbed clean, and had carefully parted and combed her short, oiled, silver curls, holding Iro's chin to keep her head steady.

'Amma, no one is going to bother,' Tebishiro had reasoned with his mother.

'They will look down upon my moonchild as it is,' Piribi had replied, clicking her tongue.

'The least I can do is have her look neat, and not like a coconut that took a tumble down the hill.'

'Please don't call her that,' Tebishiro had said in a hushed tone anxious for Iro not to overhear, *'she has to outgrow the fairy tales.'*

'One time, you believed in them too, Shiro,' Piribi had reminded him, focused on taming Iro's hair. *'There, all done! Now you're ready, aren't you, my moonchild?'*

Iro feels neat. With her sweaty palms, she pushes back the unruly white curl that had gotten free, tucking it back in its place. She had been ecstatic, stepping on the ferry in the early hours of morning, but now that she was here, Iro longed to return home and seek out the Ferrier of the ocean. Her Mino didn't look like much, but didn't Maa-ji warn her not to dismiss something by its appearance?

Here, no one smiles and every face is weary. But what intimidates her are the guards that look at her with upturned noses. Iro quickly casts her eyes downwards and walks faster to join the line. *These guards—they don't look any different from our own people,* Iro notices.

'Sentry, they are called,' her father had explained on the ferry, giving a detailed account of what she would see on the Big Island to prevent little Iro from being overwhelmed. 'Don't look them in the eye, Irah. It is considered rude,' he had cautioned. 'But do greet Madam Sergeant. She is a friend, and very excited to meet you.'

❖ ❖ ❖

'Why were they picking the stars?' she asks, almost to the little cubicle where a man with a stamp and pen sat.

'The Big Officer likes to eat them. Now quiet.'

Eat? The spines? Iro shudders, suddenly scared of this Big Officer.

'One permit for the little one, please,' Tebishiro says to the guard when their turn comes, counting coins in his palm with a furrowed brow before handing them to him.

The man nods gruffly and goes behind the iron grill, writes something down, and proceeds to tear the thick yellow paper.

'You.' He motions to Iro to come to the window. 'What's your name, little miss?'

'Iro,' she replies, hesitant, wiping her sweaty palms on her shorts. 'It's not "Miss."'

The guard and Tebishiro exchange an awkward look before he puts a wax stamp over her paper.

'He knows, Irah,' Tebishiro intervenes, an embarrassed smile spreading across his face.

'Uh...here you go, Miss Iro.' The guard waves the little paper in front of her.

Now, Iro had never had any sort of a document that held her name, and she is, at the moment, in utter awe of the sweeping manner in which her name is written, and the glistening red wax still a little warm to touch at the bottom of the paper. She doesn't hear her father thanking the guard, or them moving ahead, mesmerized as she is by this paper she has in her hands. Nor does she notice the woman in front of her as she walks into her.

'Now where would you be running off to, little miss?' the woman asks.

Iro can only gape at her.

Crisp and shining, Odette stands at the entrance of the island, wearing a uniform different from the ones Iro had seen on the sentries. She isn't tall, barely a hand over her Ma, but holds herself in a dignified way that lends her an intimidating appearance, and she speaks with an authoritative manner that would make Old Man Ehri look like a cowering mouse. Iro already likes her.

'To the bakery... Miss.'

The woman peers at her before bursting out laughing, a genial, joyous laughter like Cana's.

'I see you've met Madam Sergeant.' Tebishiro comes to stand beside Iro, 'I'm sorry, Madam. She is just excited to visit.'

'She's quieter than what you've told me,' says Odette, handing over her notebook to one of the guards and turning to look at Iro who stands fidgeting, 'Well, let me take you to the Bakery then, Miss Iro.'

❖ ❖ ❖

Iro is stunned, setting foot on her grandmother's island. She had heard a lot about the city, but hadn't expected to—no, she didn't know what she had expected. The people here, they had sunburnt gold skin, unlike the ivory sand of her home, her Maa-ji had said. And there were parasols! So many parasols in so many colours! Women walked the promenade in huge skirts that swished with every step they took, cotton and lace put together in beautiful, intricate patterns. Iro wished to take some luxurious clothing like the women's back home for her mother. She would surely love it.

But she doesn't see these uniformed men with shining rifles that her Maa-ji had warned her about, and that worries her. '*Think of the spirits there, my moonchild. That island is full of them. They watch over Shiro, and now you as well...*' Piribi had whispered to her before Iro climbed down their house's stairs.

'Irah. We're here.' Tebishiro draws her attention away from the ladies with parasols and the island spirits.

The Sergeant is holding the door with tinted glass windows open for them, beckoning them inside the Bakery. 'Come on in!'

The sweet aroma hits her face as Iro walks in, and Tebishiro lets out a laugh seeing her expression. She is openly gawking at the vast array of baked goods on display behind a glass wall, and beyond that, a man with hair the colour of bark stands, waving at them with a wide grin.

'Morning, little miss. You must be Iro.' The man leaves his counter to come and greet them, an infectious grin immediately putting Iro at ease. His words are a little broken, as though he had only recently begun to learn their language.

'It is her treat today, Mr Baxter,' Tebishiro says proudly.

'Well then, take anything your heart desires,' Mr Baxter says, happily hopping behind the counter and spreading his arms wide.

Iro is certainly spoiled for choice today.

❖ ❖ ❖

A feast is laid out in front of her as Iro contemplates what to eat first. She sits on a high chair with her bare feet dangling in air, and upon a polished wooden table are a vast assortment of baked goods, two sorts of lunches on one platter, a huge stack of cream rolls on another, and many more she hasn't ever seen the likes of. Beside it all sits a bone china kettle from which the Sergeant pours her tea that smells of flowers.

Her sandals sit neatly by the door, along with her little linen bag on a little bench, but not the coin purse. No, that she keeps safely tucked in her inner shirt's hidden pocket. It would remain hidden if only Iro would not continuously pat it for assurance.

'No one here would steal it from you, little miss,' Madam Sergeant whispers conspiratorially, 'not as long as I'm here. Now eat without a worry.'

Iro nods at her silently and picks up a roll filled with cream, and takes a bite a little too big for her tiny face.

A little away from their table sit Mr Baxter and Tebishiro, deep in discussion. Mr Baxter places an assuring hand on Tebishiro's shoulder with a gentle smile, bringing out some paperwork and carefully explaining it to him. Iro sits observing them, curious to know what they are talking about.

'Madam? Can I...can I take some of this for my Maa-ji and Ma? I'll pay for them,' she rushes to add, ears turning pink.

'Call me Odette.' Madam Sergeant smiles at her. 'Little Miss, from what I see, it's all yours anyway. I was right here when that sweet vendor came. You're a clever little thing, aren't you?'

'You don't look like the uniformed men. Why do you work for them?'

The Sergeant looks taken aback. 'I joined their army because there was no money. When I will have money, I won't need their job,' Odette answers with a wistful smile.

'My Baba also works here for money,' Iro says. 'Once our Poi grows, he wouldn't have to come here.'

'And what about you? Would you like to stay?'

'Not where the spirits are.'

'Spirits?'

'Right there.' Iro points to the tree where the ladies with huge skirts sit, before going back to eating.

The Sergeant looks around surprised, and wonders whether the girl is bluffing. She had heard Iro was blunt but crafty.

'Where are these "spirits", Iro?'

'They're my Maa-ji's ancestors. They watch over Baba whenever he comes here.'

'And you can see these *ghosts?*'

Iro puts the roll back in the plate as daintily as she can, and levels the Sergeant with a measuring gaze. 'Madam, I have lived for eight long years, and I know ghosts aren't real. But the island spirits are.'

Odette almost snorts. She does talk like her grandmother. 'Have your eight years been very long, Miss Iro?'

'Very,' Iro says with a sober face, and Tebishiro and Mr Baxter, sitting a little away from her, struggle to hold back their laughter.

'Irah—' Tebishiro interrupts, sending her a warning look. Iro simply goes back to eating her rolls.

'Okay. Will I be able to see your spirits?' Odette asks her.

'Maybe. You'll see them at night. I haven't seen one, so I don't know. Maa-ji says that they are as tall as trees and glow like stars. They will sink the island when they want to.'

❖ ❖ ❖

Iro has her arms full of treats and books as she carefully makes her way back to the stone pier while Tebishiro talks animatedly with Madam Sergeant, carrying the heavier parcels. The rush hasn't begun yet and they will be able to get a good spot.

'Miss Iro? I shall be seeing you soon.'

Iro nods furiously, an unfamiliar, shy smile making its way to her face, and carefully boards their little boat, waving at the Sergeant.

Unbeknownst to them, their every move is being watched. The man at the pier nods his head in their direction, signalling the second guard, who whispers something to his lieutenant.

They've found the girl with the mermaid in her lagoon.

THE GABLED HOUSE

Tebishiro left his house at the crack of dawn as always, lugging along two huge baskets. He was going to board the ferry today. After dropping Iro at home, Tebishiro had walked up to the village chief's makeshift office at his house, where Old Man Ehri was tending to his new crop of Rhododendrons. In the familiar gruff manner Old Man Ehri had, he struck an agreement with Tebishiro to allow him to take his ferry every day, if only Tebishiro promised not to let Iro anywhere near the pier. Old Man Ehri would not be responsible for a child going missing. Thc Big Island was a scary place. If only Old Man Ehri knew Iro would be attending school over there.

Tebishiro had, momentarily, agreed to the arrangement. He would not let his little girl partake in matters meant for adults. She needed to live like a child.

❖ ❖ ❖

Mr Baxter and Tebishiro are chatting away, both working to set up his stand before Mr Baxter takes his place behind the glass counter. The man has a habit of waking up as early as three in the morning to open his Bakery's kitchen, and by eight, he is ready for sales to begin.

Too caught up in their conversation, they don't take notice of the two guards who come to stand in front of them.

'It will take another few minutes for the shop to open,' Mr Baxter says to the guards with a welcoming smile. 'If you are willing to wait, I shall have your order out shortly.'

'You are Tebishiro?'

The guard's curt tone catches them off guard.

'Is something the matter?' Mr Baxter intervenes, standing in front of Tebishiro.

'He has to come with us.'

'Where?'

'The Governor-General's house. Sir has asked to see him,' the guard says tersely, shoving Mr Baxter aside and grabbing Tebishiro's arm, taking him with them onto the carriage.

Mr Baxter does not wait to lock down his shop as he sprints to the pier. He needs to inform Odette immediately if there is to be any chance for Tebishiro to get out safely.

❖ ❖ ❖

Tebishiro trembles as the motor carriage pulls into the driveway of the gabled house on top of the hill. It is just as majestic as the stories he has heard. He is at a loss. What has happened? What did he do? And why are his hands not bound? The Governor-General doesn't care to meet even the ones from the subordinate house, let alone him.

The guards don't utter a word. Instead, they simply motion to Tebishiro to walk in through the glass doors of the mansion where two bearers stand waiting with silver trays.

With unsteady steps, he walks ahead, unsure of what he is supposed to be doing.

'Wipe your hands and face,' the guard who had pulled him by the arm says impassively, handing him a wet towel from the tray.

'The Big Officer does not let anyone meet him till they aren't spotlessly clean.'

Hesitant, Tebishiro obeys, and follows the man down a well-lit hallway.

'Sir? he ventures. 'Why does he want to see me?'

The man gauges him with a stern face, his expression telling Tebishiro to be quiet. He walks with a strong gait and does not bother to meet anyone's gaze. As they come to stand in front of a heavy oak door, the man pulls Tebishiro back, speaking in a low tone. 'Listen to me. I don't know why he would ask for you. These officers don't talk below their peers. But whatever he says, comply with it for now.'

'Am I going to be sent there?' Tebishiro asks, rooted to his spot.

'If he wished to, you already would have,' the man replies, peering over Tebishiro's shoulder. Taking a step ahead, he knocks on the door, entering with Tebishiro behind him when a calm voice beckons them inside.

Tebishiro is taken aback by the Governor-General, a stark contrast to what he had imagined him to be.

❖ ❖ ❖

Behind a large gleaming desk, there sits a man in his late thirties, with the kindest face Tebishiro has ever seen, and yet the coldest gaze that terrifies him. Governor-General Wallis is a man of few words with a keen eye for detail. No older than Mr Baxter, he is neither a craven sort of a person, nor an old one as word floats around. 'Charming' comes to mind when one looks at this man, Tebishiro thinks.

Without looking up from his papers, the General waves his hand. 'Sit.'

The guard looks at Tebishiro, directing him to the plush chairs in front of the desk.

'Can you understand me?' Governor-General Wallis asks.

Tebishiro nods hesitantly. In the years he has worked with Mr Baxter, he has picked up the latter's language, and Mr Baxter his.

'Good then,' he says with a genial smile, a terrifying contrast to his frigid stare. 'What's your name?'

'...Tebishiro.'

The Governor-General scoffs. 'You're fortunate I'm not my father, *Tebishiro*. He was rather temperamental. That name would have immediately sent you to—what do you people call it? *The Dark Place?*'

Tebishiro remains silent, not daring to cast his gaze upwards.

'You might be wondering why you've been brought here. Selling meal parcels does not truly make a family fend for itself today, does it? How many of you are there?'

'...four, Sir.'

'You can speak up, you know.' He smiles warmly at Tebishiro, 'You will find me to be more amenable. I have a proposition for you. Join my forces.'

'Sir?' Tebishiro stutters.

'Join my army. Live here in the barracks with your family just like the rest of the sentries and soldiers. You will have a steady pay, a roof over your head, and that girl of yours can study. Iro, isn't it? You *were* looking to have her admitted to the school over here?'

Tebishiro looks at the guard who stands behind him for help, any help. The Governor-General knew of his family.

'In turn, I ask only one thing. Hand over that mermaid your daughter is hiding.'

A mermaid? Tebishiro is baffled. No one told him anything about a mermaid.

'Sir, I don't know who has been telling lies about my family, but there is no mermaid my Iro has been hiding. There are no mermaids in these waters, let alone near my Iro.'

Governor-General Wallis simply smiles at him.

'I am, what you may call, a purveyor of precious artefacts. A habit I picked up from your own land, I'm afraid. The nobility on the mainland is quite hospitable. And they scramble to be in the good graces of the Empire. Amusing, isn't it?' Governor-General Wallis grins. 'But I have seen things that would stun you. Bring me that thing your girl has kept hidden in your lagoon, and live here in peace. It is certainly better than that hut you live in.'

'But Sir—'

'Or you can simply join the ones working at the prison.'

Devoid of a choice, Tebishiro nods.

❖ ❖ ❖

His feet feel leaden as Tebishiro makes his way back to the Bakery, clutching a parcel and walking beside a quiet Madam Sergeant. The ink on his fingers leave smudges on the coarse brown paper crumpled beneath his hands. He did agree to this, but at what cost?

Was there even a creature that Iro had, or had her and Piribi's grand fables landed them in trouble?

Odette found him inside the Subordinate House, where he was being measured for his uniform. She saw Tebishiro go through the very process she had years ago. Necessity made them do unspeakable things.

Neither utter a word as Mr Baxter meets them halfway, worry etched on his face.

'What did he want?' he asks Tebishiro.

Tebishiro, tired and defeated, shrugs and holds out the parcel and his appointment letter. Mr Baxter purses his thin mouth, neatly folding the letter and placing it back over the parcel.

'Come with me. Leave it inside,' he says, putting on his cap.

❖ ❖ ❖

They walk for a long time, reaching the other side of the island where the old cemetery lies. Tebishiro never came around to this side of the island, and is baffled by the number of nameless headstones that dot the grass.

'My house is too far from here, but each morning, I take a longer route just to walk past this. Do you know what this is?' Mr Baxter asks.

Tebishiro shakes his head in denial.

'When the officer bigger than Wallis turned his gaze to this island cluster, he sent ships full of uniformed men who had never seen terrain like yours. The contact between these people ended in great tragedy—one you're too familiar with. But these graves, they belong to those men whom they murdered, destroyed, plundered.

'You know what it says?' Mr Baxter says solemnly, standing in front of an old, unnamed epitaph upon which lichen has begun to grow.

'He glanced into our world to see a
sample of our misery.
Then turned away his languid eye, to
drop a tear or two.
And die.'

Mr Baxter reads the epitaph, his gentle voice marred with sorrow. 'I know, it sounds a little grim.' He smiles sheepishly. 'But the message... I couldn't quite shake it off.'

'I don't understand....'

'What it means is, there is no one out there to watch over you. You have to think about yourself and what is good for you and your family. I don't know what the Governor-General said, and I dare not ask, but I know you. Do not let him coerce you. Don't let him put your family in danger for his fancies. He doesn't care about any of it. Just his own position.'

'I'm not—'

'Just think about it,' says Mr Baxter. 'I do have something to ask. The guard inside the Governor's house said Mr Wallis was furious when he heard your name. Why?'

Tebishiro stands still as a rock. Can he trust Mr Baxter?

'This island—the Big Island, or Wallis Island, named after usurpers, holds a name far older than the one your officers gave it. Tebishiro, the island that gave birth to the first man, Yul. I am named after my Ma's and ancestors' island, Mr Baxter. And that identity threatens the Big Officer.'

Mr Baxter stays silent. 'And you will still join them?'

PIRIBI

Iro hides behind Cana, peeking as Tebishiro and Piribi stand across each other. Between them sits a brown, half-opened parcel, holding a uniform like the ones Iro saw on the guards at the jetty. Does it mean that Tebishiro is one of the uniformed men now?

He pointedly avoids looking at Iro, his features twisted in agony. Nor does he ask about the mermaid in his lagoon. How could he? Whatever Iro was making a play of, or believing to be a mermaid, Tebishiro cannot hand it over to the Big Officer.

'It's decided then,' Piribi finally says. She doesn't look at the parcel, her mouth set in a thin straight line.

'Amma—' Tebishiro tries, but Piribi walks out of their house without glancing back.

'Irah, go with your Maa-ji, okay?' Cana says, her face just as pained as Tebishiro's. Iro leaves. Her Ma and Baba needed to talk and they didn't wish for her ears to pick up on their sorrows.

❖ ❖ ❖

'When did you last see your Mino, Irah?' Piribi asks softly when Iro joins her on the beach. Cana had told her to leave. They had matters to discuss.

'A week ago,' Iro replies. 'She hasn't been here since that day.' *The bakery and her admission,* Iro need not say.

'Find her, Irah.'

'Maa-ji?'

'You think I won't hear it, but I do,' Piribi says grimly. 'I see people in the lagoon at night, casting their nets to catch her. There are talks here. I wouldn't be surprised if someone on the Big Island knows about it as well.'

'She is hiding, Maa-ji. I can't find her.'

'We must.'

'Mino!' Iro calls to the ocean, her restless eyes searching the water for any sign of her creature.

'Mino! Please! Maa-ji, ask the great god Tarai to bring her here.'

'Tarai doesn't work as we think, little one...' Piribi tugs Iro down gently, both looking dejected.

❖ ❖ ❖

They do not go back to the house that evening, taking comfort in simply sitting and watching the sun set. Soon, they see the moon and the bright star overhead. Yul and Tuya must be watching them.

The water has started to touch their toes, waves pushing over the barrier and bringing in more sea creatures. But not Mino.

'Irah...' Piribi gently shakes the girl who has nodded off, lying with her head in her lap. 'Get up. Let's go back.'

She looks up sleepily and gets up, brushing off the ivory sand that clings to her hair.

Plop.

Iro looks up, wide awake now.

Plop. Plop. Plop.

'I hear it!' Piribi exclaims, getting up to join Iro at the shore, narrowing her gaze. A small round head, no bigger than Iro's, breaks the surface, and small, beady eyes gauge them before swimming closer.

Iro lets out an ecstatic laugh before taking off, sprinting into the water to meet Mino halfway. 'Maa-ji! Tarai listened!'

Piribi stands in shock and reverence of the creature from her ancestors' fables whom her granddaughter treats like a playmate. Trembling hands gently touch Mino's wrinkled skin, and Piribi lets out a wondrous laugh. Mino is just a youngling of the Ferriers of the ocean. *Ferriers of those who are lost to the ocean.*

'You finally found your pig with a fish tail, Irah,' says Piribi, pulling Iro's arm to loosen her grip on Mino. 'Please don't wrestle her.'

'But you said she's a true mermaid.'

'I say a lot of things...' Piribi brushes her off. 'Now, what do we do? How do we make your Mino get home safely?'

EHRI'S FARM

The street leading up to Old Man Ehri's house always emits a sweet fragrance of flowers and honey. For who could imagine a man as sour as Ehri would churn out the most mouth-watering of delicacies? A part of it he keeps for himself, a jar for Piribi he prepares as he does each turn of season, and a large glass burnie he sends to the gabled house.

He had kept a branch of the Life Tree when it was cut, installing it in his empty yard as a young man of nineteen when the older Governor-General Wallis employed people to cut it down and get him timber. The branch he had planted grew into a mighty Jarul right there in his yard, and by the time Ehri brought home his bride, he had a thriving honey farm.

Thickets of Jarul trees now grow around the little hillock, keeping his home—the only one not built upon stilts—away from prying eyes. A host of birds mill about Ehri's head as he sits in his garden, removing wax from the honeycombs and placing the sheets in his homemade machine that slowly spins as the bee-eaters living in the hollow of trees that line up all the way to Ehri's house try to peck out bees that are stuck to the honeycombs.

That's when his assistant comes around, bowing his head in greeting in front of Ehri's wife's memorial stone before sitting down, observing Old Man Ehri.

'This week's collection, Chief,' his assistant announces, pulling the heavy coin purse out of his satchel. 'Might be one person less from now on.'

'Why?'

'Tebishiro joined *their* ranks. They say he was taken to the Big Officer's house on the hill and came back with a uniform.'

'Piribi's boy?' exclaims Old Man Ehri.

'Word has spread fast across Enmei.'

'Not Tebishiro,' Ehri counters with a thoughtful look in his eyes, standing up to get the jars. 'Piribi's boy would never join the swarms unless coerced.'

'He will be stationed as a sentry at the officers' barracks from today onwards. Will also take his family with him, it seems.'

Ehri harrumphs. It only meant the Big Officer wanted to keep Tebishiro where he could be monitored. Why? Old Man Ehri is confused. Could word from Enmei have reached the Big Island? Would the Big Officer truly be interested in whatever that little menace has been calling a mermaid?

'See this?' Ehri says, showing the assistant his jar full of honey. 'It's lighter than the one before, but will still taste just as sweet. The bees might have to travel far and wide, strain, and yet will collect dew from wherever they can.'

The assistant gives Old Man Ehri a vacant look.

'Give the boy time. He is doing the best he can, given the strife,' Ehri says. He needs to talk to Tebishiro.

❖ ❖ ❖

Old Man Ehri walks up the roundabout path to Poi, adamant about talking to Tebishiro. But he doesn't expect to see Piribi and Iro huddled by the shore, talking in hushed tones over something that looks like a large lavender potato bobbing in the water. He almost scoffs aloud. Iro still has a death grip on the *thing* in the water.

So the creature was real. Not a mermaid, but the creature was very much real.

He had to do something about it.

THE SPIRITS OF OLD

The soldiers prepare sturdy little boats, with Tebishiro helping them. Their large ships would break trying to cross the barrier at Enmei's reef. He doesn't know where they're set to sail. The Dark Place, perhaps? Maybe they are bringing back some prisoner, or carrying a message to be rid of one. Tebishiro knew of them too. *The Big Island dimmed the lighthouse whenever prisoners were sent to the sea.* They didn't want their new people to see them. The Big Officer chose to keep his atrocities hidden and his people ignorant.

Find that thing that child has been keeping in her lagoon, and get rid of it, Governor-General Wallis said tonelessly to the team he was sending to Enmei. *I don't want any form of rebellion, not even from any of their young ones. You can't build a workforce like this.*

Sir? The soldier asked in doubt.

Keep them in line. Fables breed hope. Find this mermaid, and if the girl interferes, get rid of her and Tebishiro as well.

❖ ❖ ❖

Tebishiro looks like one of them now, with his brightly dyed red cotton jacket, boots and crisp white trousers. He doesn't carry a rifle, no. Those were reserved for the officers. But he is issued a shiny, freshly lacquered baton. Piribi had refused to look at him, busying herself in Poi's kitchen since the early hours while he had readied to leave for his new job as the lighthouse guard. Nor was he greeted with familiar warmth upon the ferry. Old Man Ehri had given Tebishiro a once over before letting him board.

And now, Tebishiro feels hesitant to go back home. It's a rare blue moon tonight, and the people of Enmei would be gathering at the little open amphitheatre they reserved for festivals. Not Tebishiro, no. He was made to stay on duty at the officers' barracks till his second shift at the lighthouse began.

Tuya is shining brighter than ever, Tebishiro murmurs. Is it her joy for the festival, or could it be a warning, he doesn't know. But the glowing night sky would be the perfect time to catch whatever creature the Governor-General wanted.

Could it be? Tebishiro sees the boats douse their lamps. He can't tell where they are going. He needs to find them.

❖ ❖ ❖

Madam Sergeant stands on the pier, observing them. Wallis Island is eerily quiet at this hour, with most people already retiring for the night. The jetty, even more so. She catches sight of Tebishiro, trying to look as though he was engaged in the task. Soon, he will leave for his night duty by the lighthouse, being the lone watchman stationed there. Should she leave with them? Should she reach the island before them and alert Tebishiro's family? She had heard the conversation between the Second Officer and the Governor-General the day before.

Soon, the boat master blows the shiny wind whistle, and

raises his arm halfway straight, signalling to the boat bound for Enmei to pull out of the pier. On cue, as decided, the boats disappear into the night.

But then Tebishiro turns to look at her, and takes off for the lighthouse to get to the higher ground. *He knew.*

❖ ❖ ❖

Gathering her belongings, Odette walks out of her quarters at the jetty, and makes her way back to the subordinates' barracks. Most of the street lamps have been blown out by strong gusts of evening wind and the lamplighters have already gone back to their quarters.

Worry lines etched on her face, she does not notice the faint blue glow that lights up the path beside her. She carries on ahead, as does the blue glow till she sees her shadow upon the paved street. Alert, Odette looks up from the path, and stills.

Around her stand translucent spectres as tall as the trees, each giving out a faint glow. They are everywhere—from the jetty to the bakery, to the lighthouse where she's certain Tebishiro can see them too, to the path leading up to the Governor's house. *The spirits of old...* Odette reminisces her conversation with little Iro.

The spirits of the natives simply stand at their spots, swaying gently, emitting a soft hum so low one needed to strain their ears to listen.

Odette's legs give way. Slowly, she tries to get up, but just beneath her hands, the whole island begins to tremble.

THE FESTIVAL

Piribi and Cana help each other tie strings of orchid blooms in their neatly braided hair, taking great care with the delicate flowers. Cana had decided to wear the thin chain with a single pearl strung through it, her only precious item, around her neck and wore a brightly dyed attire. But the atmosphere in their house is tense.

'I'll go find Iro. You finish getting ready, okay?' Piribi says, walking out of the house and carefully climbing down the ladder.

The night of the festival has been clear for many moons, but tonight, even the starry sky feels ominous. Piribi feels uneasy, seeing Cana look out of the window once more, waiting for Tebishiro. He won't be coming back home tonight, and Cana and she must attend the festival by themselves. But it's always Tebishiro who lights their leaf boats with offerings. She knows what Cana is thinking. Is this how they take Tebishiro away from them? *Is the duty just a ruse? Will Shiro be sent to the Dark Place?* She wonders if Yul and Tuya can sense their restlessness.

In the distance, Iro is hunched over her boat, observing the lagoon, dressed in her best clothes, definitely already having ruined them in the sand. Piribi cannot accompany her. This is a journey Iro must complete alone.

'Great gods Moïco and Tarai...' Piribi whispers as she begins to place stones in a single line, creating a path to the ocean as she has always done for Tebishiro, shakily placing Malacca roots beneath them. 'Guardians of the skies and the mighty sea, Myia and Mite, we give your Ferrier back to you. In return, guard the children of Yul and Tuya as you had sworn.'

'Let's go now,' Piribi says to Cana, her joints creaking as she gets up. 'I don't want to miss the acrobats.'

'But Amma, we can't go alone.'

'Of course we can. Watch me!' Piribi brushes her off. She can't have Cana questioning her or trying to find Iro. Not right now. 'You know her. Irah would already be trying to mingle with the pantomime actors. Remember the fright she gave you last year? Sneaking onto their boat and whatnot. Little magpie...sees anything shiny and tries to go after it,' she says fondly, taking out her small embroidered coin purse and rummaging through it. 'Chal.' *Let's go.*

Cana reluctantly follows her mother-in-law outside, keeping her eyes peeled for Iro. But she leaves the leaf boat by the door.

❖ ❖ ❖

'We have a situation.'

Old Man Ehri's assistant announces backstage at the festival, brushing his long silver wig away from his face. He is a shimmering beacon in the white robe with hundreds of little mirrors stitched on, all set to play Tuya for the first time, but the actor supposed to play his Yul hasn't yet returned from his duty at the stone pier. 'I can't go out there without a Yul.'

He opens the curtain to take a peek outside. Surely, the entire island of Enmei along with visitors from nearby islands are gathered in the amphitheatre, excited for the play to begin. 'What do we do?'

'Would you shut it about your Yul?' the organizer, one of Piribi's close friends, shouts. 'My Totemo has abandoned his costume and Myia is missing! Find me someone for Totemo!'

❖ ❖ ❖

Walking proves to be difficult for Old Man Ehri. The chief of the village drags his feet through the dark night as his heavy fanned tail trails behind him—not for the set stage and the amphitheatre where people of Enmei wait for the play to begin, but a hillock that lies just within sight of the green light of the Big Island's lighthouse. He has come up with the most hare-brained of schemes, but it should suffice.

'Ah the things I do for this village!' cries Old Man Ehri, sweltering beneath the blue costume as the ribboned tentacles hang limp by his face, weighed down with sweat and humidity.

Old Man Ehri looks pathetic. He *feels pathetic.*

He is going to be late for his performance. His shrimp suit, a far cry from what Myia is supposed to be, glitters in the night. He had spent a whole year collecting mother-of-pearl shells, cutting them with a meticulous precision and sewing them onto the light blue fabric. The great blue prawn was supposed to be majestic, wasn't he? How could Ehri go up on stage just like that?

Huffing and puffing, Ehri climbs the cliff upon which the island's torch is lit, making sure everyone below at the festival can see him. From where he is, they look like colourful specks down there, milling about the small space, unbothered by the heat. He stands in front of the torch, puffs out his painted red cheeks and heavily powdered face, and bellows, so loud it echoes over the crowd.

One by one, the crowd turns to look, mesmerized, before the commotion begins to rush towards him.

'Myia!' the crowd chants. 'Myia has shown!'

The great blue prawn has returned to the land.

Old Man Ehri can only hold his spot for a few more minutes, sweating profusely at seeing the crowd charge towards him. He turns his head to the east, and sees two tiny boats, one definitely belonging to Tebishiro's menace of a child, trying to reach the very edge of the lagoon. He casts his gaze a little ahead, and sees, to his horror, a shining boat belonging to the Big Island steadfastly making its way to Tebishiro's home.

It won't take them long. And then, he sees something unusual. A bright green light emerging from beneath the Big Island and heading for the soldiers' boat at too fast a pace. *What is that?*

But he can't wait. He only has a few moments till the soldiers disembark, and he needs to draw the crowd to them.

So Old Man Ehri lifts his heavy cotton tail and starts running downhill to the beach.

THE GREAT BLUE PRAWN

Without the lamp on her Dongi to guide her, Iro bobs in the lagoon, waiting for the familiar hum and bump below her boat. It had become quite the signature style in which Mino announced herself. Iro needed to work quickly. Her Maa-ji had said there wasn't much time.

'Come on out, you silly potato!' Iro mutters, bending to splash the water, hoping Mino would be lured to it. She kicks away the small wad of sea grass now tangled in her feet that she had kept ready to lure her pig mermaid.

'And what would you be searching for there, girl?'

Iro lets out a squeal, surprised by the gruff voice. 'Barfi wale uncle?' she says, shocked to see Old Man Bilik quietly pulling up in Tebishiro's donga boat behind her.

'What? You thought you could just cross over the barrier?' he says, mouth set in a frown. He flings a strong jute rope towards Iro, and ties the other end to his own. 'Tie this to your boat. You won't be lost to the sea if you remain tethered. I will pull us over.'

Iro looks at him sceptically, and then at the rope.

'You want that weird pet of yours safe, right? Well?'

'She's not my pet.'

'Nah...she is your *mermaid*,' says Old Man Bilik. 'Imagine my disappointment, finding your purple blobby pet instead of a magical sea maiden. Now tie it. Hurry!'

And he does. You see, Old Man Bilik had, as a young boy, been a rather excellent deep-sea diver, fishing out squids from the bottom of the ocean effortlessly before being lured in by the decadence of sweets. He had then traded his family's squid business for opening a small sweet shop, but a dispute with Old Man Ehri led him to give up the shop. He had, in turn, defiantly started conducting business on the pier just beside Old Man Ehri's ferries. He was rusty now, but diving into the quiet lagoon without a ripple on the surface to give him away was a comparatively easy task.

Yet, he isn't prepared to come face to face with whatever this little girl was hiding, a shiny flipper near the barrier between the ocean and the lagoon giving it away. A frame like someone had combined a yam and a fish, this creature is unusual and... adorable, if he were to be honest. He reaches out with one arm, but the creature only burrows beneath a crevice even more. It is terrified of him, he notices.

He wonders whether the creature would come to the boats if it saw him.

Iro looks first at the rope now swimming in the water and then at Old Man Bilik, and sits down in awkward silence. She won't tie it until it's needed, she decides.

This had turned rather interesting for sure.

❖ ❖ ❖

The lagoon is silent, with all the islanders on their way to the amphitheatre. Iro wanted to see the men on stilts once more, but they'll have to wait. Bored, she tears off little strips of sea grass, chucking them into the water. Soon, she feels a little bump beneath her boat, followed by little plops. Of course. The sea grass trick worked as always.

'Mino, let's go!' she says, reaching into the water with her short arms, trying to pull Mino up into her boat, but she keeps slipping out of her grasp. The Ferrier of the ocean is too heavy for Iro's small frame to lift.

'Get in the boat, will you, you great big potato?' Old Man Bilik huffs.

Diving into the shallow water of the lagoon, he pushes Mino up till she can be pulled up by Iro. 'I'd make so much money if I sold you to them...' he whispers, earning a glare from Iro.

'Uncle just help, will you. Come on, Mino!'

At last, Mino is secure inside her Dongi, and Iro pats her head affectionately before feeding her sea grass. Her wrinkled skin looks even more crinkled in the lamp's light, and Iro wonders how long her Ferrier will last being out of water.

'Now what?' says Old Man Bilik, climbing back into his boat. In the quiet, the only sounds are of the bobbing of little boats.

With a resolute expression, Iro raises her arm to the sea, a world beyond her lagoon that her little Dongi could never cross.

'Ah I knew this was stupid! Take this,' he says, throwing a long rope once more towards Iro, 'and tie it to your boat.'

'Dongi.'

'What?'

'It's not a boat,' Iro declares, pulling the rope out of water and tethering their boats with a sailor's knot she learnt from Tebishiro. 'Dongi.'

'Fine! Dongi!' he says exasperated, 'Where did you learn to tie it like that? They teach you that at that school in the barracks?'

'I haven't *been* to the school. Baba did.'

Old Man Bilik nods to himself. What in Myia's grace has he agreed to do?

❖ ❖ ❖

They paddle as soft as they can, not disturbing the stillness of the water. Mino is anxious to go back to the sea, so she fidgets.

'Not that far, Mino. We'll get you home, won't we? Then all the guardians of the sea and great god Tarai will take you back to your home. Home, Mino!'

'Where is this thing's home? Or are we risking drowning just like that?' Old Man Bilik asks, trying to catch his breath.

'Maa-ji says Mino is one of the Ferriers' younglings. Great god Tarai tasked them to make Tarai's guests reach the cane bridge.'

Old Man Bilik is sombre. He knows now which direction they are supposed to row in. The waves push back at the calm waters of the lagoon, making it difficult to cross.

'Hold on to your Dongi, Irah!' Old Man Bilik says. 'I can't lose Tebishiro's child to the ocean.'

'Don't worry! Myia will protect Mino.'

'Oh he would, wouldn't he...' Old Man Bilik mutters under his breath. He had left the pantomime's *Myia* alone with his Totemo costume, and he knows Old Man Ehri will start a fight with him the next morning for abandoning him. They are about to have a theatre without his Totemo in their thirty-one years of playing their characters. *Once, just once, let me play Moïco, and I'll be the one casting you into the sun, Ehri,* Bilik vents. But then he hears a bizarre, croaky bellow, and Mino curls up inside the boat even more.

What in Moïco's blessed name is that? He can't concern himself with odd sounds. Right now, the potato mermaid needs to be sent home before the guards come searching for her.

They try to release Mino into the water, but the giant waves prove to be a challenge.

'Tarai! Moïco! Myia! Come and help us!' Iro shouts, nearly toppled over by the waves save for being tethered to the bigger boat. But before them, the ocean seems to sway. The great shining ships that are moored, which sometimes rained fire, now drift off from the Big Island's pier, and the green light of the lighthouse flickers violently before shutting off. Something is going on at the Big Island. *Myia...*

The pig in the water swims to the bottom of the ocean and wakes Myia... Piribi had said in one of her disjointed tales. Is her pig mermaid *that one?*

'Iro, is Tebishiro at the festival?' Old Man Bilik asks, jolting her out of her thoughts.

'...he's over there,' Iro points to the now dark lighthouse, scared.

'Let's get your pet to safety first. Tebishiro will come back soon, okay?' he assures her. *Tebishiro will be back.* And with all the strength his feeble frame has, Old Man Bilik rows, steadily getting them to the brink of the open sea.

'This much is safe. Now your Mino can get back,' he says, putting their boats beside each other. Together, they try to push Mino out and into the water. Mino seems to sense it, and eagerly tries to roll over. The moment her flipper touches the water, she dives in, swimming fast away from Iro.

'Mino!' Iro calls out to her, but Mino doesn't care to look back. She holds the edge of her Dongi as Old Man Bilik gently drags their boats to the shore. Does the Ferrier of the ocean truly not care?

'Irah, come,' Old Man Bilik says, trying not to look at the tiny blip out in the open sea.

'Wait!' Iro exclaims, getting out of Dongi and sitting on the shore as Piribi and Tebishiro did each time the green light went out. 'Great god Tarai, watch over my Mino in your waters. Lead her home.'

They soon see the green light from the lighthouse travelling the open sea, circling the ocean. One could mistake it for lights dancing if it were not heading straight for Mino.

'It's not the lighthouse,' Old Man Bilik whispers before running back to the water.

'Mino! Swim faster!' he screams.

The green light travels beneath the water as Iro and Old Man Bilik look on, lighting it up, till a massive fanned tail breaks the surface. In a blink, Mino's head disappears in the waves, and the light stills, flitting in circles where Mino is supposed to be, till it diverts, gently moving in the direction of the Dark Place. The great guardian Myia came to take the Ferrier of the ocean, guiding Mino home.

❖ ❖ ❖

At the very moment, the soldiers' boat is almost at the brim of the east side of Enmei, when they spot something glowing underneath their boat.

'What is that?' says one soldier.

'I can't see. What is it?'

'The boat! Get out! Something is below the boat!'

The waves rise, and with it, so does the boat. Myia? Could it be? A spectral shadow of a man as tall as a mountain stands out of the water—a man with a fine beard and eyes which seem to glow underneath the moonlight. Or is it the ocean playing tricks on their minds?

Is it Myia? The ancestors of old? Yul? Or is it the great god Tarai looking over Yul's children? But with one huge lash, the boat crashes upon the coast, splintering into pieces.

❖ ❖ ❖

When dawn breaks, word reaches Enmei that the Big Island has been abandoned. They say a massive quake split the island in two, others say the great god Tarai had enough and decided to end the reign. Yet, none besides the Big Island felt the tremble and the earth shattering. How could they? The people of Enmei were too busy running after Myia to notice a quake.

One by one, the men in uniforms and their kin leave the Big Island. No word is heard of the Big Officer, but those who reach Enmei say he left for the mainland upon his shining ships to meet his superior. And the Dark Place? No one knows what will happen. The forces still stay, but they say it isn't for long. Piribi says the great god Côl shall rest for a while now.

Mr Baxter and Odette don't leave. They choose to come to Enmei with Tebishiro. What Tebishiro witnessed upon the Big Island, he doesn't say, but he kneels and touches the sand with his forehead when he sits on Piribi's path, saying silent prayers for his guardians. Later, he sits with Cana upon the shore, holding his family's leaf boat—the only wish boat on the island left to be sent—and places their wishes in it before pushing it off into the sea. They pray that great god Tarai finds it and listens.

For the first time, Tebishiro smiles.

And Iro? She receives a little surprise from her civets when she does find them in the morning after letting go of a friend.

❖ ❖ ❖

Old Man Ehri reaches Poi in the morning, coming out of his hiding place from the kobo bushes where he has abandoned his precious suit. He did draw the crowd to the beach, but the shining boats never reached Enmei. So Ehri ran across the heavy sand and into the forest to get away from the people. He would never hear the end of it if they knew.

But there is much to do and he cannot stay hidden forever, so he comes by the lagoon to strike an accord with Tebishiro. He, along with many others, is left without work since the Big Officer left. Standing outside of Poi, he can see the Big Island split in half. He goes to stand behind Piribi who sits in her usual place by the stilts, stringing another charm for Iro, this one holding mother-of-pearl shells that look a little too familiar.

'It's a blessing,' Piribi says, threading a large needle. 'I told you the guardians don't abandon us, didn't I? See how Tebishiro claimed its name back.'

Old Man Ehri hums in approval. It takes time, but stolen names always find their way back. *Enmei is just as changed as the Big Island now, isn't it,* Ehri wonders. How quickly life bounces back into routine as if nothing has changed.

'She has something for you.' Piribi gives him an amused look, chuckling to herself as she gets up to leave.

Just outside the little hut, Old Man Ehri sees Iro, and walks up to her all chuffed.

'So your school is gone?' he says gruffly.

Iro just shrugs.

'And your Baba is—'

'Safe,' says Iro. 'He doesn't have to go to *the Dark Place* with chains.'

'Ah. Well, do you know who saved everyone yesterday?' Old Man Ehri asks, chest puffed with pride. Surely, she must have figured out. Piribi's grandchild was a smart one after all.

'Of course!' Iro says with a grin, holding out a fanned tail with mother-of-pearls stitched on, the rest of the blue suit torn by and hanging from the mouths of Beyan and Koio. 'It was Myia.'